Jean,

For your unwavering support . . . thanks,

Jeff

Permanent Vacation

A CW McCoy Novel

Jeff Widmer

Published in the United States in 2018 by Allusion Books, Sarasota, Florida. Allusion Books and the Allusion Books colophon are registered trademarks of Jeff Widmer.

http://jeffwidmer.com

FIRST U.S. EDITION

For Karen, Katie and Mike

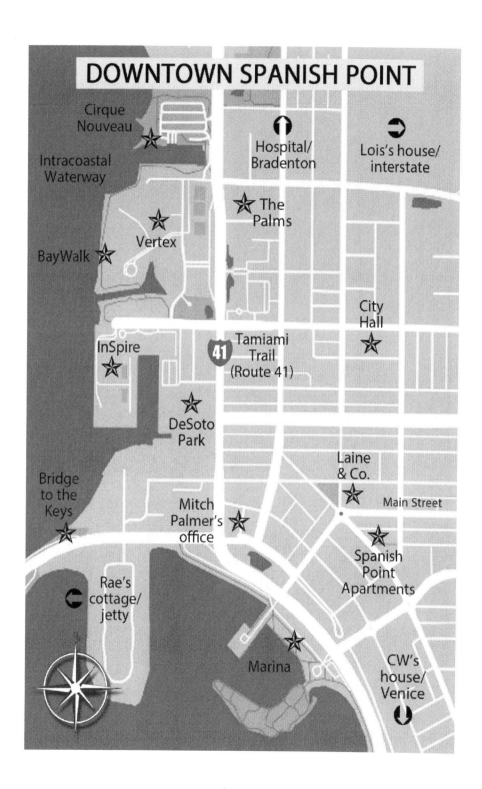

DOWNTOWN SPANISH POINT

Cirque Nouveau

Intracoastal Waterway

Hospital/ Bradenton

Lois's house/ interstate

The Palms

Vertex

BayWalk

City Hall

InSpire

Tamiami Trail (Route 41)
41

DeSoto Park

Bridge to the Keys

Laine & Co.

Mitch Palmer's office

Main Street

Spanish Point Apartments

Rae's cottage/ jetty

Marina

CW's house/ Venice

1.

IT HAD RAINED forever. With two months left in hurricane season, we'd suffered two indirect hits and a half-dozen soakers, including the latest tropical storm, which stalked Spanish Point like an internet troll.

Noah would have been impressed.

When people think of Florida storms, they picture high winds and palm trees doing the hula. But most of the damage lately had come from water. And with relentless development filling the coast, the water appeared everywhere. Gushing from storm sewers, flooding shops, stripping beaches of their sand.

The state depended on those attractions, and the media that hyped them. Good publicity attracted tourists who flocked here on holiday before deciding on a permanent vacation. Buy a piece of paradise and live the dream. They're happy. We real estate agents are happy. It was a win-win situation.

Until it poured. As it had for the past week.

Which made my decision to ride the Kawasaki on slick roads a questionable one. But, I argued with myself, I had cabin fever, it was my last weekend before reporting to my new agency and the sun coast had negotiated a temporary ceasefire with the weather. So of course I headed for the water.

Cirque Nouveau looked the polar opposite of Rae Donovan's former bar a few miles down the road. Where the old place had clung to the pier like a barnacle, this one looked polished, themed and expensive. Its architecture consisted of a train car built on an enormous scale, with the entire western wall open to the bay. At the entrance, a big top announced the name with the words "The Greatest Show on Earth."

The interior hosted a collection of circus memorabilia, from stuffed parrots to gilded parade wagons to a miniature clown car—a supersized tribute to a nostalgia no one could remember.

While the place appeared full—floral shirts and strappy sandals *de rigueur* for the touring class—I had no trouble spotting Rae. Towering over the crowd, she wore a red tuxedo jacket with velvet lapels and a bowtie. Juggling a half-dozen bottles, she poured drinks for a bar overrun with millennials.

She greeted me with a shout and leaned over the bar for a one-armed hug and a buss on the cheek, attracting the attention of a pair of crackers a few stools away.

"What brings you to my humble abode?"

She had a voice like rust. I'm sure the crackers had no trouble hearing it.

"Time to see your new digs." I took in the space—the wait staff in shorts and Hawaiian shirts, TVs hanging like acrobats over the bar—pointed to the speakers in the ceiling and shouted, "Where's the country?"

"We traded Hank for Jimmy Buffett. What's your poison? I've got a special on mai tais, or would you prefer a margarita?"

She twirled a stemmed glass. My lower lip buckled.

"Yeah, I know. It's pretentious as hell, but the high prices more than make up for it."

I slid onto a seat near the end of the bar and ordered a beer. In the mirrored wall, the bay swelled with moonlight and bashed the seawall. The restaurant sat along the Intracoastal Waterway a few miles north of the marina. The few boats tied to the dock banged their hulls against plastic bottles the owners had strapped to their craft. Never a good sign.

"Don't you miss your old place?" I asked. "I was sure you'd rebuild."

She ran a cloth over the bar top. "Can't afford to, not in this town."

I took in the fake palm trees, the circus posters, the trapeze dangling from the ceiling. "You all right, working for someone else?"

"Hell no, but my brother's the boss. Some things never change."

"Eddie owns the restaurant?"

"It's a franchise, or can't you tell?" She raised a hand. "And before you say it, it beats unemployment. Speaking of which, when do you start the new job?"

"Monday."

"Nervous?"

"About returning to work for Casey Laine?" Over the summer, I'd worked for a boutique agency until a violent death forced me back to what agents affectionately called factory real estate—the rules, regulations and steady paycheck of the largest brokerage on the Gulf Coast. Rae wasn't the only one who thought almost any work beat unemployment.

She compressed her lips, her version of a commiserating smile. "I hear she's a tough old bird."

"Let's just say she's exacting."

As illogical as it seemed, I surveyed the restaurant to make sure my new boss wasn't listening. Not that the queen of real estate would condescend to a tourist trap like this. What I did see was an abundance of circus décor—posters of the Ringling Brothers, a high wire net spanning the ceiling—and the two crackers appraising us with wide eyes and knowing grins.

They looked in their early twenties. One had skulls and demons tattooed over bulging arms and hair that looked like a paintbrush. The other had a long snout, like a bottlenose dolphin. As if to call attention to the shape, he'd pierced his septum with a horseshoe hoop whose double balls resembled frozen snot.

Shelving the bottles, Rae wedged a pair of pilsner glasses between her fingers, worked the tap and slid the beer in front of the guys. When she returned, I tilted my head in their direction and, despite the clatter of silverware and plates, lowered my voice.

"Who are those beauties?"

"Paying customers. Try not to piss them off."

"When have I ever pissed off anyone?"

With her fingers, she ticked off a litany of names. "The mayor, the chief of police, every boss you've ever worked for. And let's not forget Junior Darby, our resident firebug."

Skulls and Bottlenose smiled—at least they'd retained most of their teeth—and raised their glasses, as if thanking us for the round.

Rae nodded. I dipped my head and took a sip—after another ninety-degree day, the foam felt cool against my lips—and massaged my forehead. "Can we talk about something easy, like disarming North Korea?"

"Sure. What'd you do to your hair?"

"What do you mean, what did I do?"

She chuckled. It sounded more like a snort. "Are those highlights? I thought you hated blondes."

"I don't hate blondes. I used to work for one."

"She's the one who went after your boyfriend, right?" Rae must have read a sour look on my face. "OK. How about politics and religion. They're safe."

I glanced at the TV screens. Three were broadcasting sports but a fourth, tuned to the local twenty-four-hour news channel, featured a candidate promoting prayer in school. "I'd skip religion if I were you."

Rae swiped the bar with a towel. "OK, you want to talk politics? How do you explain this? The city approves Tommy Thompson's plan to build this monster development along the bay without a peep, then backs it with taxpayer money. It doesn't matter if you own anything in the way, like a restaurant that draws in the tourists. It's grow big or go home."

"You're starting to sound like the mayor."

"That is the mayor," she said. "His favorite tagline. Face it, the man's gaslighting us."

"The city has to do something with the old performing arts center."

"Everybody knows this whole strip from here to DeSoto Park sits below the waterline. The Gulf's rising, we're getting more rain, bigger storms, and the city's handing out permits like jelly beans at Easter." She tipped her chin to indicate the dock, where the bay took another crack at parking the boats inside. "At least we have a seawall. Not that it'll matter once the city levels this place for the new boat launch." She snapped a bar rag. "All for the greater good."

"It is what it is."

"Catchy expression," she said. "One of yours?"

"A friend of mine." I sighed. I hated these discussions, as if newcomers weren't entitled to the same benefits we transplants had acquired.

Rae hooked a thumb in the direction of InSpire, the newest condominium on the bay and the one I'd start selling next week. "Not to put too fine a point on it, but you pedal that stuff, right?"

"Those towers are built to withstand a Cat 4 storm."

"If they don't sink."

"That's why God invented engineers."

She gave me her famous fisheye, the one that said I was full of something other than beer.

"All right," I said. "It bothers me, too. You happy now?"

She dried a glass. "Question is, are you?"

"I'd be happy with a change in leadership."

"You mean once the mayor and his rubberstamp are gone."

"Please don't get me started on Phil Cunningham."

She pointed to my glass. "Freshen that?"

"It's half-full."

"Always the optimist."

"No, thank you." I checked my phone. It was almost two. "I'd better sign off." I glanced at the pair holding down the end of the bar. They waved, pointed to their beer, then at me. I forced a smile, pressed a palm over my glass and hoped that would end any late-night flirtation.

"Last call!" Rae yelled and worked the length of the bar, settling everything from memory, no tabs even when the customer had ordered food, cash flowing into the register like a river. When she returned, she placed a fresh glass in front of me and shook her head. "They say you look like you could use another."

I glanced in their direction. Both nodded.

"Tell 'em thanks but no thanks."

"They're desperate."

"They're creepy."

"Like my nephew," she said. "More confidence than brains."

"You have a creepy nephew?"

"Ryan's a little footloose since he was let go from his job. You probably read about him. The cops caught him trying to scale that condo tower you're trying to sell. Then get this. Last week he got busted for racing his bike on Baywalk." She pointed toward the surging Intracoastal. "That promenade or whatever the marketing people are calling it these days."

I shook my head. "Is he all right?"

She snorted. "You kidding? He's an adrenaline junkie. He loves the attention. Now he wants to surf the jetty off Spanish Key."

"That's nuts. The riptide will tow him halfway to Mexico." I knew that breakwater, a heap of broken stone with pockets deep enough to swallow a boat. "I thought the city declared it off limits."

"That only encourages him. He calls it performance art."

I would have called it stupid but he was Rae's nephew and I didn't want to offend. "You said he was let go?"

"From that new development the mayor just approved."

That new development would be a showcase for my new employer, and a moneymaker for her agents.

"Did Ryan work for Thompson Partners?" I asked.

"For a sub, doing site prep."

"Nobody gets laid off in this economy, especially in Florida. What'd he do? Or shouldn't I ask."

"He said some numbers didn't add up in some report and when his boss wouldn't listen he went over his head."

"What numbers."

She waved the bar towel. "Some study the sub was doing."

"Who'd he talk to?"

"Somebody in city hall. His boss found out and now he can't find a job."

The restaurant had cleared except for a waiter and waitress stacking chairs on tables and the pair anchoring the near end of the bar. They'd stopped smiling at us. I leaned toward Rae. "You think the mayor had Ryan fired?"

"He's Mr. Business. I wouldn't put it past him."

I glanced at the nearest TV. Leslie Ann Roberts, the star of the Gulf Coast News Network, stuck a microphone in the face of Charles Palmer and asked him about the long rebound from the Great Recession. For the better part of the summer, Palmer had seized every opportunity to promote the stock of Thompson Partners Inc., the developer of DeSoto Park and its next phase, the thirty-four-acre ribbon of property that stretched between InSpire and Cirque Nouveau.

Palmer claimed status as the region's leading attorney and wealth manager. Of more importance to me, he'd sired Mitch Palmer, my former boyfriend, the man who'd dated my former boss. With the noise of the bar, I couldn't hear the elder Palmer but I could read the crawl. Given the rapid growth along Florida's Gulf Coast, he had a buy recommendation on TPI stock.

The interview switched to Phil Cunningham. The footage must have been shot before the storm blew through, because the mayor appeared relaxed in short-sleeves and slacks, a sunlit bay polishing his sandy hair. Echoing Palmer's assessment, he rattled off a list of seventeen condo projects in the downtown core alone that had started or were in the planning phase. With a radiant smile, he spoke of more to come.

The segment ended with Cunningham's trademark line, the one he was using in his campaign for the Florida statehouse. "It's good to see cranes in the air."

It felt odd to watch the mayor promote Tommy Thompson's company, no matter how generic his remarks. By all accounts, except the official ones, Cunningham had an affair with Thompson's estranged wife, Susan, the head of the Spanish Point Visitors Bureau. Pregnant, she'd been shot and killed in a carjacking gone terribly wrong. Cunningham blamed a mythical war on tourists. I blamed the mayor. I had no idea what Tommy Thompson thought.

The screen faded and programming switched to a roller derby match.

Rae collected tips and swiped the bar top with a rag. "Could be your chance to finally nail the bastard."

It took me a second to reorient. The state attorney had declined to file charges. The mayor had an alibi, an election-eve campaign event. He had a hundred witnesses, including me. "I tried. I got stonewalled."

Rae's eyebrows danced, a sure sign she wanted to rope me into something dicey. "You want to talk to my nephew."

"Can I ask why?"

From her back pocket she extracted a phone. "I'm texting his info. Meanwhile." She snapped the bar rag and yelled to the guys at the end of the bar, "Guys, we're closed. Time to hit the road."

The pair tossed some bills on the counter and bumped the back of my stool, not hard enough to trigger a fight but enough to make a point.

I heard the words *bitch* and *dyke* overlap, as if they couldn't get their stories straight.

Without turning, I gave the pair a one-finger salute.

Shoving the cash into the register, Rae said she'd been called worse.

"Have you seen them before?"

"No," she said. "You?"

"I've seen their type."

"And they've seen yours."

"Independent," I said.

"Ungrateful," she said. "Hell hath no fury like a young buck scorned."

"Poetic," I said.

"The hell with poetry. You don't still carry, do you?"

"Not since I left the force."

Over their shoulders, the pair treated us to a hard stare before slipping onto Baywalk and into the night. I asked Rae what I owed, laid some money on the bar and doubled the amount for a tip. After having to deal with the likes of those two, she deserved it.

She used the back of her sleeve to wipe her forehead. I offered to walk her to her bike, a classic Indian Chief with a 1,200cc engine. It could hit eighty-five in third gear and peel the skin from the roof of your mouth. The image brought a wave of jealousy.

"It'll be a long walk," Rae said. "Damned thing's in the shop again."

The jealousy faded. "You need a lift?"

"You bring the Kawasaki?"

Compared to modern machines, its 500cc displacement seemed underpowered, but the bike could leap tall buildings in a single bound when pushed. "Always," I said.

"Should only take us a week to get home."

A man who looked like a homeless person emerged from the kitchen and pulled down the shutters.

"The cook," Rae said. "In case you change your mind about a date."

We waved and left through the backdoor, reaching the lot as a car backfired. The hair on my arms stood at attention. I'd parked the Kawasaki close to the building, an old habit to keep it from getting bumped. The only other vehicle in the lot was a dark Jeep Wrangler with black-rimmed tires and a tow winch in front. The engine was running but the lights were off.

"You still have that cottage on the keys?" I asked.

"Until some developer tears it down for a high-rise, no offense."

I offered my helmet. She raised her hands.

"There's no visor," I said. "You can still pick the bugs out of your teeth."

"Tonight," she said, straddling the back, "I'm going commando."

I donned the headgear and threw a leg over the seat. She looped her big arms around my middle and we crunched over the loose shells of the parking lot. I'd pulled dead even with the Jeep when it lurched forward, giving me a second to hit the brakes and spill us or try for the highway.

It was a no-brainer. Cranking the throttle, I flashed before the Wrangler, my stomach lurching as the front wheel threatened to go airborne. But the bike held its ground and, in the mirror, I watched the Jeep disappear in a cloud of blue smoke. Between the close call and the break in the rain, I gave in to the urge to run at full bore, the G-force stretching my insides as we raced south along the Trail.

The guys in the Jeep must have taken offense. Within a block, the Wrangler caught our tail, weaving in and out of the lanes to play catchup. At one point, the Jeep edged so close I thought it would ram us headfirst into the stack of cars.

Between Baywalk and the condos, there was little room to maneuver. Flooding had reduced six lanes to two. While the rain had stopped, the right lane remained under a foot of water, judging by the wake created by the cars. If we hit the light at the bridge, we'd be sitting ducks. If we detoured into town, we'd lose speed but gain agility.

I had to turn my head to hear Rae.

"Slow down, Hoss! I want to make it to next week!"

"What's next week?" I yelled, taking a hard left for a run along First Street.

"Payday!"

We skirted the big blue office building where the mayor and the Palmers held court before blowing through the first intersection. The Jeep clung to my tail. There was no way anyone would take this route unless they were going to the theater, and those guys hadn't looked like patrons.

Time to fly. Gearing down, I redlined the machine through the next two lights, flying past the dark office of Laine & Company, hugging the traffic circle at Main so low I thought my helmet would clip the curb. The grip on my stomach told me Rae was still there. She knew the drill, leaning into the curve to keep the bike from throwing us across the sidewalk.

Even as we shot from the roundabout, the Jeep gained speed. I hit Main Street for two blocks, then doglegged to regain the Trail, followed only by the screech of tires. No car could match a motorcycle on a straight stretch and yet there it was, dogging us past the damned concert hall.

"Hold on!" I yelled. "Time for evasive maneuvers!"

Rae tightened her grip as we powered between the steel bollards that blocked cars from entering Baywalk. There was no way the Jeep could follow. With rising satisfaction I watched its lights shrink as we fled south, past the skateboard park and amphitheater.

By the time we reached DeSoto Park, we'd lost them. Leaving the walkway, I raced under the banyan trees toward InSpire and its unfinished twin to rattle the bike up the granite steps of the high rise. The restaurant that occupied the first floor appeared deserted. Through its glass walls, rows of tables with white tablecloths glowed in the exit lights. Staying here would risk complaints from residents, but the spot offered a good vantage—the better to see the Big Bad Wolf, my dear.

Below the condo, the Intracoastal slammed the seawall. Even in the dark I could see water gushing from the storm drains, forming psychedelic pools of light at the intersection of the bay and the bridge. And this from the brush of a tropical storm. What would happen if we took a direct hit?

I turned to Rae. "You all right?"

Her hair resembled pictures of Medusa with the snakes sprouting from her head. "I got to say, lady, you've got chops."

I hadn't made the license plate but the chase had angered me enough to report the bastards. Dragging my phone from a pocket,

I'd started to punch in the county's non-emergency number when an engine revved and I turned to watch the Jeep vault the steps. We had enough time to clear a leg over the bike when the Wrangler clipped the Kawasaki and launched us through the window.

2.

FOR THREE IN the morning, the nurse sounded depressingly cheerful. He looked nothing like the staff on *Gray's Anatomy*. His chin bristled and he smelled of rubbing alcohol and lime. A tattoo of a snake entwined his right forearm while his nose and ears bore holes where he'd removed several piercings. Picking glass from my face, he hummed a Dierks Bentley song, "Drunk on a Plane."

I hoped that wasn't an unintentional message.

Tweezers in one hand and a metal dish under my chin, he told me to look straight ahead and dropped another shard into the tray.

"How much of that stuff is in there?"

His glove crinkled. His eyes didn't. "You've heard of people who live in glass houses?" When I nodded, he reminded me to hold still. "If I were you, I wouldn't throw any stones." Maneuvering around the examination table, he alternated tweezers and a cotton ball with disinfectant, his ministrations annoyingly slow but touching.

He straightened to give me the full-body scan, no doubt admiring his work. Despite my position on the bench, his head struggled to reach my chin. But then, maybe that's how they designed those things.

"You play ball in college?"

The pain in my forehead seemed to double. I pointed to the cuts. "You throw darts?"

He unpackaged a bandage and leaned in for the kill when the curtains whooshed on their metal tracks and a boyish voice entered the examination room. "You're lucky you hit hurricane windows and not plate glass." The voice belonged to a man wearing a white coat, a stethoscope and the look of an undertaker. He was short and slender with a face that would never need a razor.

I pointed to my forehead, where a lump that felt the size of a grapefruit had formed. "There's someone picking glass out of my face and you're telling me I'm lucky?"

"Done," the nurse said and taped a bandage over the lump.

"Impact glass," the doctor said. Swinging the stethoscope into place, he pinched my wrist and listened to my heart at the same time. "They consist of two panes. The outer layer shatters while the inner core is coated with a laminate that allows it to flex. It can stop a nine-pound two-by-four traveling up to eighty feet per second."

My head felt as if it had been hit by said board but the doctor might give me some pain killers so I decided to be civil. "Thank you, Bill Nye."

He stepped back. His coat seemed to glow. Either he'd just collected it from the laundry or I had more of a headache than I'd thought.

I was dying to ask for a mirror but too vain to ask. "How's it look?"

"There's no craniofacial damage but there may be some small shards, above the eyebrows, mainly, that are embedded too deeply for us to reach. I can refer you to a plastic surgeon, if you like, or you could wait to see if any of the fragments express themselves on their own."

I thought about asking how glass might express itself, verbally or with hand signals, when he examined the scraped arm and leg—they burned but didn't hurt too badly—and told me I could dress. I wanted to say that I was already dressed but his comment ended the exchange. The curtains whooshed and I was left with buzzing fluorescents and a head to match. Until another voice interrupted my daze.

"Here's trouble," the voice said and I had the feeling she meant it.

Under ordinary circumstances, Officer Cheryl Finzi looked drawn and tired. She was one of the huddled masses, a single mom who volunteered for overtime to meet the mortgage. I knew this because she was my neighbor—I'd sold her the house next to mine. She usually wore too much eye makeup to hide the fatigue, which, by the end of her shift, gave her the appearance of a raccoon with insomnia.

This morning she looked annoyingly cheerful.

"What'd you do this time?" she asked. "Try to make a citizen's arrest?"

"It wasn't my fault."

"I've heard that one before." She leaned against the wall. "How're you feeling?"

"Like I just dumped my bike and my best friend, present company excluded. Have you seen Rae? How is she?"

"Broken arm and a couple of bruises. You're lucky you had a helmet."

"I offered." I still felt guilty. "But you know Rae."

"They'll hold her for observation. X-rays, CAT scan, you know, the works."

Shifting on the table sent a bolt of pain down my leg. "They're looking for signs of concussion."

"They're looking for money."

I winced.

Extracting a notebook and pen from a pouch, she asked what had happened. I told her.

"You both got lucky," she said as Charles Stover pulled the curtain aside. A fellow officer in the Patrol division, he was tall, dark and as sinewy as a player in the NBA. He'd used those muscles to good advantage when we'd worked with Habitat for Humanity, before the last hurricane. The deadpan expression said he wasn't here to volunteer.

We nodded at each other and I directed my attention to the slender box he carried in his left hand. "What's that, pray tell?"

Cheryl, who occasionally dated Charles, gave him a look as if to say, 'you think that's necessary?' But she said nothing. I couldn't blame her. She had my goddaughter, Tracy, to support and couldn't afford to play favorites.

"You know the drill," Charles said and extended the clear plastic tube of the Breathalyzer. "Pucker up."

"If you say I should be good at this. . . ."

His face creased with an attempt at a grin. "Never crossed my mind."

I complied. Checking the reading, he showed it to Cheryl, pocketed the device and left.

I looked around the cubicle for my shoes. "Mr. Conversation."

"Don't worry," she said. "You're under."

"I only had half a beer."

"If I had a nickel for every time I've heard that."

"You find the Jeep? It's got to have some damage."

"We're looking."

"Who even does that? Who runs down people for cutting them off in traffic?"

"Road rage happens everywhere."

"This is paradise," I said. "We're supposed to be immune to the stuff."

Her lips ticked sideways. "We're heading into peak season. Too many tourists and vendors in too much of a hurry."

She pulled a pack of gum from another pouch and offered a stick. Shaking my head, I returned to the visual search for footwear.

"I get it," I said, "but it was close to 2 a.m. when we left. Traffic was light, even heading toward the bridge."

Propping a pair of tanned forearms on her utility belt, Cheryl leaned against the wall. Her eyes narrowed. "Rae says these guys were half in the bag. She'd called time and they didn't show a willingness to leave. If they're anything like my ex, you turn off the spigot, you've got a fight. Think you're being dissed by a couple of women on a ride they'd give their eyeteeth for and you've got trouble."

Her explanation made sense in a macho, no-impulse-control kind of way but it didn't answer the question that had dogged me since the crash.

She tapped the side of her head. "I can tell by that look you've got something going on in there."

"Did Rae tell you what we were discussing before we left the bar?"

Cheryl shook her head in a slow exaggeration of a pendulum.

"Phil Cunningham."

"Not him again. What's he got to do with anything?"

"Rae was talking about a nephew who just lost his job because he reported a fudged report on one of their projects, the proposed development north of DeSoto Park."

"And you think the mayor ordered a hit on you?"

I raised my hands in mock dismay. My right arm, shrouded in bandages, didn't move at the elbow. "I can't say, but think about this: is it a coincidence Rae's badmouthing the richest guy in town, a guy who uses his charity for at-risk kids as a proving ground for thugs, and an hour later she's attacked?"

"Maybe they weren't after her."

That made my limbs tingle. "Where is she?"

Cheryl, who'd clamped her hands on the edge of the body armor, hooked a thumb over a shoulder. "They probably have her in X-ray by now."

I put weight on my right leg and it cursed a blue streak. Cheryl came off the wall and gripped my good arm before I caved.

"Thanks," I said. "I can manage."

"You want an escort?"

"Don't you have real drunks to bust?"

"Yeah, but as my mother would say, you look like you need minding."

I took a breath and scanned the exam room for anything I didn't want to leave behind, such as my dignity. Cheryl's concern was touching, in a brusque kind of way. The last time I'd gotten involved in one of the department's cases, the murder of several

Spanish Point real estate agents, she'd virtually accused me of dragging her into the fiery pit. Snippy. I felt glad to the gills that she'd returned to form.

My leg had stiffened. I located the shoes under a chair and struggled into them. "I should do my penance alone."

"They'll never let you see her, not if she's still in radiology." Cheryl snapped her gum, using it as most people used punctuation.

I tapped my heart and tried to wink with my good eye. "I'll use charm."

She tapped her badge. "No offense, but this works better."

3.

I WOULDN'T ADMIT it but Cheryl was right. No one paid attention to the woman with the scuffed face and a limp. But they took notice of the blue uniform and stern look that could have frozen water off the Miami coast. A few "she's with me" and we were standing outside the room with the X-ray equipment, waiting for Rae to emerge.

When she did, we trailed behind, chatter at a minimum, until the wheelchair reached her room. While Cheryl braced herself against another wall to keep it from falling, I took Rae's hand and told her I was sorry to have gotten her into this mess.

"It's not your fault those idiots don't know how to drive." Her face looked as battered as mine—I had a hard time telling the freckles from the scratches—and an inflatable splint encompassed her arm like a balloon. But her eyes were clear and her smile wide and she didn't appear to be in pain.

"What'd the doctors say?" I asked.

She yawned and tried to cover her mouth, only to bump her nose. "They won't know for sure until they get the film, but except for a busted wing, I'm ready to do cartwheels."

I took in the room, with its ports and tubes and curtain that offered as much privacy as the backless hospital gowns. "How long are they going to keep you here?"

"Who knows? They want to stick my head in a CAT scanner and bake it at 350 for an hour. I told them it's too big to fit."

I squeezed her fingers. They looked swollen. "They're trying to rule out internal bleeding."

"My head's too hard to bleed."

"Anything we can do?" I asked.

"You could swing by the house and feed the cats, although they ought to be good for a couple of days—if they don't dismantle the furniture and give it to Goodwill."

Cheryl started digging through the clothes that an aide had brought to the room.

"How many cats?" I asked.

"Five or six. It depends on the season."

"I thought you were a dog person."

"I get that a lot."

I promised to look in but drew the line at hauling twenty pounds of used litter to the curb.

"Just dump it on the beach," she said. "The tide will carry it out with the rest of the sand."

I'd heard about the erosion but didn't know it was that bad. So I asked.

"In two years," Rae said, "we've lost seven feet of shoreline, and it was only twelve-foot deep to begin with. One more soaker and I'll be living in a houseboat."

She gave me the street number, an address near the jetty on Spanish Key, and said I'd find the key under the mat.

I rolled my eyes. "Great security."

"We're living in paradise. What could go wrong?"

Cheryl snorted and pushed off the wall. I told Rae to get some rest and we headed for the gap in the curtains.

Rae called after me. "It wasn't your fault!"

"I know!" I yelled back.

"You don't mean that!"

"You're right, I don't!"

* * *

"What do you think?" I asked Cheryl as we shuffled to the elevator, the pain in my leg radiating from shin to thigh.

"I think you don't yell in a hospital."

"I mean about the guys who hit us."

She punched the call button. "You're lucky you're not wearing a neck brace."

"What about the bike?"

The doors swung open and Cheryl hit the button for the lobby. "New pipes, new paint. The tail needs a little work. You'll manage."

We crossed the stony tile of the reception area, the pneumatic doors hissing like a basket of snakes, and stood under the canopy of the medical wing, the remnants of the storm gurgling through the gutters. The sky had cleared and the sun struggled to rise above the condo towers.

Cheryl said she'd have the Kawasaki towed to a garage and asked what I was going to do now. "Just so we know where the next disaster's gonna be."

I forced a smile designed to wilt the faint of heart. It had no effect on her. "I need to check on Pap and prep for work. The city's unveiling the next phase of the DeSoto Park project tomorrow and the boss says it's all hands on deck. And I should call Tony."

"What, and tell him you dumped the bike?"

"I need to adjust the schedule."

She clacked her gum. "You mean, you're gonna bail on him again."

She knew perfectly well that Detective Tony Delgado and I had been dancing around each other for months, the main issue being whether I was too radioactive for his career.

"If you must know, we've set our first official date."

"I thought you guys already went out."

"We had lunch, if you call it that, and did a banquet, that command performance for the mayor's charity."

"I bet you're seeing somebody. Who is it? Oz?"

"He works for your department," I said. "I bet you see him more than I do."

"Didn't you guys have a fling?"

"I negotiated his lease," I said. "I didn't hack IT."

"What about your buddy Mitch?"

"His father dislikes me as much as he likes Tommy Thompson's stock."

"Tony, Tony, Tony," she said.

I didn't know where she was going so I waited.

She smacked her gum like a rubber band. "Two workaholics. There's a match made in heaven."

For months, she'd been pushing me to make a run at Delgado, so this had to be Cheryl's version of irony.

"Do you always say the opposite of what you mean?" I asked.

"Do you always do the opposite?"

She had me there. I had wanted stability and dated Oz, who made black-hat hackers look like altar boys. I had wanted excitement and dated Mitch, who managed his emotions as he did his clients' money—with an abundance of caution. Silence seemed the best policy now, so Cheryl and I spent some quality time examining the condos across the Trail. Despite the natural backlighting, the towers looked sullen, row after row of cubes stacked to the sky, most beyond the reach of the tallest fire truck in town but not the Gulf's grievous waves and wind. People thought agents here sold real estate. What we really sold was curb appeal— the appearance of luxury and the illusion of safety.

When Cheryl didn't want to share, there was no waiting her out.

"If you must know," I said, "we're supposed to meet tonight at that shack on the tip of the keys, the one where they take all of the brochure photos."

"Oh, yeah, the place where you dine with your tootsies in the sand."

I grimaced, which passed for a smile these days, and pointed to my bandaged arm. "I should call Tony about this. Unless *you* want to tell him."

She waggled both hands. "Don't drag me into your sordid affairs."

"It's not an affair."

"Then you'd better hurry up. We're taking bets at the station."

My arm and leg had started to itch and it took willpower to ignore them. "On what?"

"On whether the two of you will ever settle down."

"Out of curiosity, what are the odds?"

She yawned and stretched and I wondered how long it would be before I could move like that. "Eight to one against."

"Which side of the bet did you take?"

She cackled. "The winning side."

The parking lot appeared deserted, apart from Cheryl's squad car and an ambulance idling in a pool of its own fumes. I didn't want a ride in either, but I needed a shower, and Rae's cats would relocate the cottage if I didn't run out there soon.

I turned to Cheryl just as her radio squawked. "How about if I trade you a cup of coffee for a lift?"

Dispatch reported a disturbance at a convenience store south of the hospital. I recognized the address, a place the cops nicknamed the Stab 'n' Grab for all of the armed robberies there. Cheryl acknowledged with her position.

"Hold that thought!" she yelled and jogged across the lot, a little too much enthusiasm in her gait.

4.

"THANKS FOR NOTHING!" I called to the retreating squad car, and I meant it. As a parting shot, I added a small wave with my good arm. Recognizing a recent client, the EMTs in the idling red truck waved back. Talk about humbling.

From a tattered pocket I pried my phone. It had survived the encounter better than my leg. Punching up the ride-sharing app, I called for a car, hoping I'd get home without getting murdered. It was early but I called Pap's assisted living facility to make sure it hadn't sprung a leak and settled down to wait, which I don't do very well. To take the edge off the boredom, I checked my phone every few seconds. A bad habit that, someday, I would break. Just not now.

The screen showed a map with my location, the image of a car and its driver—a Prius and a somber-looking man by the name of Hudson—as well as the ETA. Sure enough, ten minutes later, a Prius the color of a fire engine arrived. It was still early, the sun barely out of bed, but as the car glided under the bright lights of the hospital entrance, I could clearly read the dozens of stickers that papered its bumper: "Save the Gulf," "Visualize Whirred Peas," "Coexist" printed in religious iconography and "Your Text Here." That seemed to cover the bases.

The driver, when he levered himself from the car, ran to five-five and a shade over sixty. True to his photo, he sported a doughy face with dark glasses and thinning black hair that didn't match the gray at his temples. Hobbling to the back door, he struggled for balance. I moved to put an arm under his but he waved me off.

With a slight bow he said, "Gary Hudson. I'll be your chauffeur today."

His deep voice had a hint of the Midwest.

"Thank you, Mr. Hudson," I said and slid into the back seat. Unlike the exterior, the inside appeared uncluttered, with the exception of a Darth Vader bobblehead on the dash, a tree-shaped air freshener dangling from the rearview mirror and a pair of metal crutches with loops for the upper arms on the passenger side.

Settling into the driver's seat, he adjusted the mirror. "Call me Hud. You're CW?"

"I am."

"Just you today?"

"Yup."

"You ever play basketball?"

"What's with the basketball stuff today?"

He didn't seem fazed by the tone. "There's water in the cup holder and extra cellphone charging plugs in back, in case you need them. I know a lot of people do. You ever notice people live on their phones these days?"

Talky but courteous. If we got home in one piece, I might rate him five stars.

"Where we going?" he asked, although he knew the address, since I'd entered it when booking the ride.

"Could we make a detour first?"

"No sweat, but you'll have to request a separate trip."

I fished in my pocket, confirmed I had Rae's house key and entered the address for her cottage. His phone, attached by a claw to the air vent, lit up as he accepted the fare. It wasn't until he pushed a button to restart the car that I notice the levers sprouting from the steering column and a handle like the pommel of a saddle that gave the wheel a nautical look.

He caught me staring. "I had polio as a kid. I was fine until a couple of years ago. Not fine, but I could get around without those." He pointed to the crutches. "Doctors say as you get older the symptoms come back. Maybe that's why I like driving so much, you know? Gives me the freedom to move around."

"I'm sorry," I said.

"It could've been worse. I could've ended up in an iron lung."

I hadn't heard that expression since my grandparents had raised me as a child. They'd lived through the polio scare.

The radio played a classic by Rascal Flatts. Hud snapped it off.

"You can leave it on," I said and tried to arrange my legs so the knees wouldn't jam the back of the seat.

I caught a faint smile in the mirror as he restored the music and swung the car out of the parking lot with a deft touch of the wheel. It was early and traffic on the Tamiami Trail was light, the water that had covered four lanes of the highway relinquishing two.

He kept checking the mirrors, as if he, too, were being followed. "So what brings you to paradise?"

"Work," I said, just to keep things on neutral ground.

"What kind of work?"

"I'm in real estate."

"Ah." He tipped his head in an exaggeration of ecstasy, a move that revealed a tonsure like a monk's. "Selling paradise, one lot at a time. What's your agency?"

I told him.

"That's a coincidence. We bought our place from you guys, a couple of years ago. The wife and I kept coming down here on vacation and after the third or fourth time we decided to make it permanent. Let the kids worry about filling the oil tank three times every winter."

"Do you miss your family?"

"They tell me how hot it is down here. I tell 'em, at least we don't have to shovel heat."

He laughed before delivering the punchline. I smiled. That small encouragement opened the floodgates. He was a retired civil engineer, a Boilermaker from Purdue, and the one thing he didn't understand about Florida was how people could build so close to a natural hazard that threatened to drown them six months of the year.

"Sure," he said, pointing to the rows of condos that walled the corridor to the east. "You throw a parking deck on the first two or three floors, fill in with commercial, no sweat if they get damaged. But what happens when that water sinks into the ground, goes right through the cracks to erode the limestone? I don't care how deep you drive the piles, those buildings are gonna make the Leaning Tower of Pisa look like an architect's rule."

I couldn't picture an architect's rule and the headache that had subsided made a return appearance. Pinching my forehead, I leaned into the seat.

His eyes met mine in the rearview. "You OK? You look like you just went three rounds with Manny Pacquiao."

"Is he a friend of yours?"

"Never met him. It's just that you're looking a little peaked." He pronounced the last word PEEK-ed. "You have a headache? My wife's always getting headaches. She says it's her sinuses, they act up when a storm's coming. I keep telling her she needs new glasses. You wear glasses?" He took the wheel in his left hand and began rummaging through the glove compartment. "I've got some Tylenol in here somewhere."

"No, no," I said as the car wobbled. "I'm fine. Really. Thanks."

The Prius was a lot lower to the ground than my SUV. Splashing through puddles large enough to generate waves, the car seemed to float down the Trail, the water deepening as we approached the marina.

"We'd better take another route," he said.

"There are only two. Why don't you take the north bridge to the keys."

"Yeah. These cars are great on gas but you never know how waterproof they are."

The big blue office tower, the home to half-a-dozen wealth managers, loomed on the left. Hud had cleared the intersection when the proverbial bulb lit his brain.

"Wait a minute. I know you. You're that nosy real estate lady who investigates crimes."

"Nosy?"

"Yeah, the ones the cops can't solve."

My stomach curdled. It was just the kind of talk to land me in trouble.

The Prius rolled over the bridge and across the causeway, the waves lapping at the roadside, Hud giving the vegetation a wide berth as he took the road to the beach.

"Do you think you could hurry it up a bit?" I said, thinking maybe I'd overcompensated for his handicap by mentally offering to give him a five.

We headed south, toward the narrow neck of Spanish Key, at a pace of a tourist.

"Yeah, I saw you on TV last month, when those agents got strangled. You're lucky you weren't one of them. You ever need help staying out of trouble, just ask. I hear a lot of things in this business."

"I bet you do."

"I used to do this kind of stuff up north."

"Driving?"

"I couldn't say."

I wondered if this guy had worked as a police informant, or a former cook who, ratting out his pals at the meth lab, had run for his life.

"Go ahead," he said. "Try me. Ask me about what goes on in this town."

"OK, what do you know about the new development on the bay?"

"Those towers in DeSoto Park?"

"No," I said. "The Bayfront expansion to the north."

"That's funny business."

I leaned forward. "What's funny business?"

"You know, financial shenanigans, backroom politics, a lot of rannygazoo. You've got a half-a-billion-dollar development, private development at that, and Thompson Partners gets the government to put up more than half the money. It's like that baseball stadium they built south of here. Rich owners, poor taxpayers—like Robin Hood in reverse. All of those guys—they promise jobs and feed off the public teat. I tell you, the place'll wash into the sea before the city can retire that much debt."

"Who's your source?"

"Ah," he said, and I caught a smile and a wink in the mirror. "I never kiss and tell."

"Good Lord," I muttered as we drove past the parking lot and pavilions of Spanish Key Beach. To ease the throbbing in my temple, I watched the scenery, great clumps of sea oats and palmetto screening the Gulf from the shore. As the vegetation thinned, the jetty hove into view, a thick black line that cut through the surf, the water an ugly curl of gray bashing the rocks. Motion caught my eye, then a flash of blue and white that didn't belong.

"Pull in!" I shouted.

"Where?" Hud yelled but ran the Prius along a dune and jammed the brakes.

In good weather, the jetty was a favorite fishing spot. But this wasn't good weather. Waves pounded the rock and sprayed the beach. No one would risk those waves, and I hadn't seen a rod or a boat.

Something long and pointed bobbed to the surface before vanishing beneath a wave.

"What is that?" I yelled.

"Looks like one of those paddleboards. People lose them all the time. Are we done here?" He raised his phone with the ride-share app. "You know waiting fees apply after two minutes."

He'd put the car into gear when I spotted an arm.

5.

BOLTING FROM THE car, I pushed through palmetto and sea oats to the shoreline. Waves swept the jetty, blackening the rock, flushing its cracks with foam. At first I saw nothing. Then something flashed, blue and white in the growing dawn, and a surfboard breached the surface. It was attached to a glossy black cord, and an ankle.

"Call 9-1-1!" I shouted to Hud and, kicking off my shoes, sprinted into the water.

I'd gone three feet when a wave hit my midsection, the undertow yanking my legs from beneath. Scrabbling backward, I flipped and pushed off my hands and knees to stumble onto shore.

Hud stood by the open door of the Prius and thumbed his phone.

"Hud!" I yelled. "Rope! I need rope!"

Using the car for balance, he hobbled toward the rear and worked a yellow cord from the hatch. I grabbed the coil, cinched it around my waist, told him to tie off around anything he could find and pushed into the waves. I leaped the first two and went under the third to emerge a few feet from the jetty, Hud reeling in the slack so the surge wouldn't sweep me into the rocks.

I found the surfer and board wedged into a fissure about two feet across, just above what would have been the water line. From the short hair and bare back I guessed it was a male. Reaching around his chest, I braced my feet and pulled. He moved easily at first. Then the board flipped sideways and jammed between the rocks and we stopped with a jolt.

The next wave buried us but I kept his head above water and leaned against a tide that threatened to sweep us into the Gulf. Tightening my grip, I tried to swim for shore but he wouldn't move. The surfboard leash anchored his foot. I'd have to let him go and either unhook the strap or undo the Velcro around his ankle.

Another wave hit and we went under, the rope pulling me in one direction as the undertow yanked my feet in the other. Taking a deep breath, I let it carry me, the sand scouring the cuts on my face, the water a stinging gray wash in my eyes and mouth. Grabbing one foot and then the other, I felt for the Velcro strap. It had twisted and tightened, no way to free it, but the cable release snapped with ease. Surfacing for air, I watched the board smash the rocks and disappear.

We had to move. Wrapping an arm around the man's chest, I pulled for shore. The waves gave us a final push and I dragged the surfer onto the beach and collapsed. When my breath returned, I got my first good look. His back looked gouged, his skin blotchy and red. His legs, covered with a matted pelt of hair, twisted as if he had no joints. Hud appeared at my side. We rolled the surfer onto his back. I considered CPR, but one look at his face told me the man had passed beyond help. The waves had smashed his head against the rocks, tearing an ear, crushing his nose and caving his mouth.

Sirens wailed. No Doppler effect, so they were drawing near.

I brought my gaze back to Hud. He was a civilian, so I'd expected to hear retching. But he stared at the body as if it were a mannequin, the cord he'd used to anchor me hanging loose in his hands, his palms raw from rope burn.

Chest heaving with the effort, I stood as the first Fire/Rescue truck arrived.

"You did good," I said, the words sounding like a gasp.

He continued to stare at the body.

I took him by the arm. "Why don't you wait in the car."

I got him situated in the passenger seat and asked if he had a blanket in back. Two squad cars pulled beside us, the alternating flashes of blue and red light blinding. I shaded my eyes and watched Cheryl step from one of the cruisers, Charles Stover from the other. With a full-body shrug, they settled their utility belts and approached.

"He didn't make it," I said.

Stover disappeared over the rise.

Fire/Rescue arrived in a big red truck, followed by the engine the city always sent as backup. So did two white SUVs driven by the incident investigation team. They suited up and marched down the beach, cameras and toolkits slapping against their plastic coveralls.

I put a hand on Hud's shoulder and spoke to Cheryl. "When they're done, the EMTs should check him for shock."

She nodded and, as Stover returned, motioned me toward the beach.

They interviewed us separately. I told Cheryl how I'd spotted and recovered the body. Hud was out of the car now, leaning into one crutch, waving his free arm toward the water as if describing the dimensions of a room.

"You know him?" Cheryl looked at the body, surrounded by techs and a photographer, bearded, mid-thirties, squatting for a better view.

Sunlight finally had reached the beach, bleaching the sand and surf. I looked at the battered man, a small, dark figure engulfed by a very large space. Even from this distance, his condition made me shudder. "I couldn't make out the face."

One of the evidence techs, bundled like an astronaut, told Stover she'd found what appeared to be the surfer's clothes in a backpack where the sea oak met the beach. She handed him a wallet in a clear plastic bag. Shrugging into gloves, Stover extracted a Florida driver's license and showed it to me.

"You recognize him?"

The face meant nothing, but the name struck home.

"Yes," I said, my voice so quiet it barely registered above the waves.

6.

CHERYL DROVE ME home and saw me into the house. After confirming that I had the medical supplies to change the bandages on my arm and leg, she headed back to work. No cracks about swimming in my clothes. I felt relief.

Despite the sting of the water on what were still open wounds, the shower washed the tension from my muscles. I used the gauze Pap kept in the medicine cabinet to wrap my limbs and slid into a T-shirt and shorts, with nothing touching the arm and leg, not even air. The side of my face had blackened in a spot that resembled the peninsula of Florida. There wasn't much that I could do with that, or the bigger scratches, or the lump over my eye. Concealer would only cover so much. But that couldn't compare to what Rae would experience when I arrived at the hospital with the news about Ryan.

Fire/Rescue would move his body to the medical examiner's quarters, where they would try to establish the time and cause of death. The police would call on Rae's brother, Eddie, with the worst news a parent would ever hear. Eventually, when the shock wore off, he'd call Rae, but I didn't want her to hear about her nephew's death from the cops, or her brother, who would be dealing with his own grief. If only I hadn't spent so much time at the hospital yacking with Cheryl. . . .

I made myself a cup of coffee and tried to drink it standing at the sink but my muscles wobbled so much that I spilled half the liquid and gave up, rinsing the mug and stacking it with the rest of the dishes. I hadn't been home much. The place still felt empty without Pap. He kept falling and forgetting to eat and take his medicine, and with my work schedule, showing homes almost around the clock, I couldn't look after him. I knew I'd done the right thing by placing him in an assisted living facility but the act still felt like a betrayal. Pap and Alma had raised me since I was five, since my family died in a house fire. I owed him more than a bed in God's waiting room. I missed his warmth, his very presence, even if all he did was sit in the recliner with an afghan on his lap and watch TV.

My hands steadier, I grabbed the keys to the SUV and headed for the hospital, wondering how I was going to break the news to Rae.

* * *

I didn't have to. I found her in the orthopedic wing, flying around the room, grabbing at clothes and cursing the arm cast, which kept getting in her way. Struggling into torn slacks, she said her brother Eddie had just called.

"Then the damned police called and told me about Ryan. I said, 'How does a twenty-two year old kid who lives on a surfboard drown in three feet of water?' They don't have a clue, not a fucking clue."

"I'm sorry." I gave her a hug, the cast clunking against my back.

"They said you tried to rescue him but he was already gone." She had me in a bear hug that squeezed like a vice.

Untangling myself, I held her at arm's length. "I tried, I really tried."

"I know you did."

"I was on my way to check on the cats and I saw the surfboard and then an arm or a leg. . . ."

"Hey," she said. "Just get me out of here before I do something stupid."

"Did they finish the tests?"

"The hell with the tests."

I handed her a work boot, a reminder of her bar life and a small act of defiance of the Cirque Nouveau dress code. "You sure you can leave?"

She took the boot, found the other and grabbed a comb from the nightstand. "You just watch me."

* * *

By the time we reached the SUV, the adrenaline that drove Rae from the hospital had spent itself. She slumped against the door for the entire ride. Neither of us said anything. Rae stared at the scenery, or some movie in her head. In the silence, the police scanner crackled with an endless litany of ten codes. I'd installed it for old time's sake, but now the chatter seemed obscene. Turning down the volume, I focused on the road.

In the early morning hours, Spanish Key looked peaceful, the roadways passable, the resorts quiet, their neon signs mercifully dim, as if in deference to the tragedy. The peaceful feeling didn't last. As soon as I took the turn onto Midnight Pass Road, my hands tightened on the wheel. I kept glancing at Rae but she didn't move. When we rounded the curve just north of the jetty, I took my foot off the accelerator but didn't brake.

"Stop," she said, her voice flat and thick. "I want to see where it happened."

I pulled onto the spot where Gary Hudson had parked. Rae powered down the window and stared. The beach looked different in full daylight, the sand bright against the glossy black of the rock. It extended into the Gulf like a broken finger, accusing the waves of a cruelty it could only accept. I couldn't, and as I watched Rae's eyes roam the shore, I knew she couldn't, either.

I patted her knee.

She nodded. "Let's go."

* * *

Rae's cottage sat between a wall of condos and a gated community where teardowns sold for millions. The outside was unassuming, a wooden hut hunkered down among palmetto and sea oats. The walls were cypress, probably harvested from the marshland near the Everglades. Old Florida, with a metal roof, porch with a rocker and a cooler to the side.

The interior couldn't have been more than a thousand square feet, but she'd used it well. The colors were bright—the walls white, the floors green, the doors a federal blue—and the furnishing spare—plank tables, wicker chairs, an anchor with a rusting fluke bolted to the wall. No knickknacks or other clutter.

Standing at the window, Rae rested the cast on the frame and surveyed the Gulf. I dispatched a silent prayer of thanks that we couldn't see the jetty from here and asked if I could get her anything.

"Water," she said without turning.

The wood had started to show through the paint on the kitchen floor, but the bead board walls looked crisp in a glossy white. I reached into the round-shouldered refrigerator for water when she yelled "use the tap." I found a glass in the cupboard and listened to the faucet hiss, my hearing as sensitive as the nerves in my arms and legs.

Handing her the glass, I sat on the edge of a striped ottoman and waited.

She kept her eyes on the water, as if wary about its next move. "Ryan," she said. "Ryan Edward Donovan, after my brother, Eddie."

"I'm sorry. I got there too late."

"At least you were there."

"Why was he out in the storm?"

"Who knows? He's like his father at that age."

"You said he lost his job. Started to tell me some of this in the bar but what exactly did he do?"

She turned, her face dark against the backlight of the window, and folded the cast under an arm. "He worked for an outfit called Gulf Coast Drilling. They do geotechnical evaluations—test borings, soil samples, seismic tests. All that stuff to make sure the building won't collapse."

"Was he qualified for that?"

"He just graduated from the University of Florida. Civil engineering. He didn't want to come back home—he and Eddie didn't always get on. He wanted a job with one of those big firms trying to keep the ocean out of Miami, but this one came up first."

"Friends? Girlfriends?"

"Who knows? Kids never tell grownups anything."

She would know. A former teacher who tended bar in the summers, she grew to like the nightlife more than grading papers, or submitting to an administration with more testosterone than brains. She also knew how to operate construction equipment and had built a good portion of her old bar, a wooden fishing shack that became a favorite hangout for boaters, misfits and anyone passing through town. Spanish Point's premier thug, Junior Darby, had torched it as a way to keep me from tying him to the murder of Susan Thompson. I'd failed to nail him, or the man I considered his handler, Phil Cunningham, for the crime.

I looked past her toward the Gulf. Palm shadows flickered across the sand. Now that the tropical storm had moved west, waves brushed the beach like a gentle hand. This was private land, acres of it, coveted by every developer in Florida. Rae's house, her little piece of paradise, wouldn't last. The condos would force march her into the sea.

I said, "You never did say how he lost his job."

"Probably smart-mouthing his boss. You know how that goes."

Unfortunately, I did. She did, too, so I shouldn't have been surprised by her question.

"Maybe you could look into it."

"I'm not exactly plugged in," I said. Or welcome at police headquarters.

"How about that boat bum you hang out with. Walter? Doesn't he run a security company?"

I tried to relax a jaw that had automatically clenched. "He's not around."

She raised a brow as swollen as mine.

"He took off in his boat, trying to outrun the hurricane." I raised a hand. "And before you ask, I've called every marina from Naples to Pensacola and no one's seen him, or the *Mary Beth*."

"You try his phone?"

"Marina, house, cellphone. The calls go to voicemail and I keep getting this message that he hasn't setup his mailbox."

"Maybe he swamped."

A pang radiated from chest to feet. "It's my fault. I drove him away."

"I thought you said he felt cooped up with his lady friend, Lois was it?"

Lois Danforth was the retired nurse who'd wanted Walter to trade his sailboat and black lab for a riding mower and homeowner dues.

"I didn't think she was good enough for him," I said. "And then I took her dog."

"You look like you're the one who could use a home."

"I should be going. Big day tomorrow. The city's unveiling plans for the redevelopment of the Bayfront—the vertical groundbreaking, as my boss likes to call it." I rose. "You need anything?"

She gave her head a shake.

"What are you going to do now?"

"See Eddie as soon as I clean up. Then back to work."

"Hair of the dog?"

She raised the cast. "It's a busted wing, no big deal. As long as I can pull a pint, I get paid."

"Won't Eddie close the bar?"

"Hell, no. It's a chain. He just owns the franchise—more like renting it. With those corporate types, you don't show, they hire a college kid who'll work for tips."

She gave me her profile, as if undecided about whether to look in or out. Her voice, when it came, was as dark as syrup. "He was young and reckless. Who isn't at that age?"

I slid my arms around her big shoulders, gave a light squeeze and stepped back to view her face, the swollen forehead, the greenish bruises. Her seawater eyes roamed the room but found no rest.

"He talked a good game, but even he wouldn't surf near those rocks," she said. "Not in that weather. Just look into it, OK?"

"OK," I said, knowing there was no way it would ever be.

7.

SUNDAY NIGHT OFFERED the first decent weather we'd had in a week, the tropical storm having hauled its cargo of rain to the Panhandle and beyond. The sky was clear. My mind wasn't. I should have been happy. Lieutenant Tony Delgado was handsome, athletic and smart. One of the best detectives in the Spanish Point Police Department, he cleared cases at an enviable rate without logging a single ethical lapse. After months of denying the attraction, I'd scheduled our first formal date.

And yet I felt far from romantic. My limbs hurt and my face still resembled a dartboard. I didn't feel like socializing. I didn't even feel like eating. But I'd cancelled on Tony so many times I feared if I didn't go, he'd stop asking and I'd be alone forever and that's when women collected cats and named them after characters in a Bronte novel.

So we agreed to play tourist for an evening and meet at a restaurant called the Outer Jib where, in addition to the specials, the chalkboard listed the sunset time. Perched on the rim of a barrier island, the place offered a view of the Gulf without a single condo or hotel in sight. Adding to the tropical ambiance, white sand embraced the tables and umbrellas shaded diners from the glare of twilight.

I arrived a little later than arranged and we bussed each other's cheeks, mine burning with schoolgirl swoon at the touch of Tony's lips. At six-feet, he was one of the few men I could look up to. In his late-thirties, he had the broad shoulders and the trim waist of a basketball player who swam the Ironman for fun. High cheekbones, eyes like dark chocolate, black hair with the hint of a wave and a thread of gray—he had a magnetism that animals would envy. If his face had a flaw it was the small dent in the middle of his forehead and the thin white scar that divided his chin. But after last night's collision with a glass wall, who was I to talk?

Tony wore a white Oxford, sleeves cuffed to the elbows, khakis that held a military press and loafers—his idea of casual. He held a chair for me that offered the best view of the water and put his back to the wall, giving him a panoramic view of the clientele, exactly as I would have done in my policing days.

He crossed his legs and clamped a hand on his ankle.

I gave him big eyes. "You're not wearing socks."

"My feet get hot."

"Interesting look."

"I'm headed to the Hamptons after this."

"Honestly, on anyone else, I'd call it an affectation."

He picked two menus from the table and handed one to me. "How's the face?"

"How does it look?"

He smiled. "Honestly?"

"Don't answer that."

Rustling silverware and menus, I tried to focus on the specials but my attention kept drifting toward the Gulf. Diners dug their toes in the sand. Boats glided, gulls wheeled and the sun made its endless trek toward the horizon. Over the sound system, in a song that hit number one the year I turned thirteen, Faith Hill urged us to just breathe. I took in the clean air and the laughter and tried to feel a peace that passed all understanding.

Judging from Tony's expression, he read the emotions that crossed my face and, God bless him, said nothing, choosing to point out the virtues of various dishes.

I set my phone on the table, face down to be polite, and did the very thing I promised myself I wouldn't: pump the detective for information. Starting with what he knew about the drowning, and the thugs who'd tried to push Rae and me through a wall.

Lowering the menu, Tony folded his hands and made a sound as if someone had shoved the Serenity Prayer under his nose.

"Is this your idea of a romantic date? A full-court press?"

There it was again, another annoying reference to basketball. I took in some air and told my pulse to stop dancing. "Maybe I should have stayed home with an improving book and an icepack on my head."

He lifted the corner of his mouth in what, for him, constituted a smile. "If I say anything at this point, it can and will be used against me."

"There is that possibility."

A waitress appeared wearing a glossy smile and the tightest top and shorts this side of a waterpark. To his credit, Tony kept his eyes on me. A prince among men. When the waitress toddled off, I made a silent vow to treat him as more than a disposable source.

The vow didn't last. No sooner had the iced tea arrived than I asked about the next step in the Ryan Donovan investigation.

"I couldn't say."

The sun hovered over the horizon like a broken egg. I wanted to shade my eyes but that would look like a sign of weakness, so I squinted at Tony for effect. "Couldn't or won't?"

"Another detective pulled the case."

I tried to raise my eyebrows but it hurt.

He leaned back to give me the level stare. "You know I can't discuss it."

"Just tell me if you think he drowned."

"You were there."

"Did anybody help the kid into the water?"

He shook his head. "Too hard to tell. You saw the body."

"I was afraid of that."

"Is that all?" he asked.

"All I want to know?"

"All you're afraid of."

The sun nestled on the horizon. I let out the breath I'd been holding.

"You're concerned about the accident," he said.

"My bike? That was no accident."

I'd gotten a partial tag—the guys in the Jeep hadn't tried to disguise it, maybe because they thought I'd be too dead to testify. I asked Tony about that. When he hesitated, I raised both hands in a gesture of surrender.

"You're either a bad source or a very tolerant date."

The hint of a smile returned. "Tolerant or tolerable? All I can tell you is what'll be in the press release."

I leaned forward only to dip an elbow into a pool of condensation from the tea. "Come on, who are they?"

Tony raised a hand and began to recite in that clipped version of speech that cops reserved for courts and the press. "The Jeep's registered to a John H. Bates, sixty-nine, retired colonel, U.S. Air Force. Served in Vietnam. Jack Bates died last week in a memory-care unit in Venice. His grandsons have been living with him, two brothers, nineteen and twenty-one. Venice police are looking for the Jeep."

Crap, I thought. Rae had served an underage drinker. I kept that knowledge to myself. "Either of them have a record?"

"They've both appeared in juvenile court."

"And the records are sealed."

He slid a photocopy of two licenses across the table. "Are those the guys?"

Surprised he was so prepared, I tapped the paper with an unvarnished nail. "Skulls and Bottlenose."

"Glad you're on intimate terms."

I pulled the paper for a closer look. "Can I keep these?"

He shook his head.

"I'm glad that's settled. What are the odds the mayor's behind this?"

He gave me the kind of stare I'd seen on alligators. "Why should he be?"

"You remember Junior Darby, the mayor's poster boy for rehab?"

"Hold that thought," he said as the food arrived—pulled-pork barbecue and fries for me, burger and salad for Tony, and refills on the tea.

I crinkled my nose at the salad. The motion hurt my forehead. "We have a motive yet?"

"We?" Carefully, as if peeking under a bed, he lifted the bun and applied catsup. Then, reassembling his dinner, he licked a finger.

I lost patience waiting for the reply so I ate. The barbecue had a nice tang. So did the pickle.

"When you find them," I said, "I'd like a private talk."

"I bet you would." He took a bite of salad and blotted his lips. "I'll save you the trouble. They'll claim you cut them off in the parking lot. We'll charge them with aggravated battery with a deadly weapon. Too late to make a DUI stick."

He gave me the long stare. He'd pulled the sheet and knew Charles Stover had breathalyzed me and was waiting for a mea culpa. I wouldn't give him the satisfaction.

"Since when does that warrant a high-speed chase that ends in a face plant on a window?"

He started on the burger.

"So there's no chance that Cunningham was involved."

Tony's head rotated slowly from side to side. "You need to watch what you say."

"Why? He was involved with Susan Thompson. He's married to Casey Laine, who owns the biggest real estate shop on the Gulf Coast. He's running for the statehouse. The scandal would have put him out of business."

"Show me the proof."

"Just because he didn't pull the trigger doesn't mean he didn't order her death."

He rimmed the iced tea glass with a finger. "Law enforcement officers rely on evidence."

I heard the implication. "You mean since I'm no longer a LEO, my theories don't count."

"We need more than theories to make it stick. You know that."

"And if no one's willing to rock the boat?"

Tony ate. "How's your rider?"

"Rae? She has a broken arm but no major cuts or concussion."

He sipped tea and watched me. "And you?"

"Frustrated. Angry. Does it show?"

"Hardly ever." Reaching across the table, he pinched one of my fries. "Mind?"

"Help yourself."

Considering the grilling I'd given him, I interpreted the gesture as intimate, one that gave me a little more leeway.

"Is there a connection between the drowning and the crash?"

He chewed in a way best described as methodical. "Nothing more about investigations, OK? This is supposed to be a social event, not a news conference."

"OK," I said. "What about Walter Bishop? Have you heard anything?"

"No. You?"

"I have called every blessed marina from here to Alabama and no one has seen the *Mary Beth*. How can a boat just disappear?"

"You really want an answer?"

"No." I felt my stomach knot.

"You try his phone?"

"The man still has a clamshell. He hasn't even set up his voicemail."

Giving the impression of a grin, Tony said he would ask the Florida Highway Patrol to be on the lookout in case Walter had come ashore, but there wasn't much more he could do.

"I am grateful, even though I don't show it sometimes."

A smile breached his lips. "Sometimes?"

I felt a warmth I hadn't experienced in years. Not that I would reach across the table, take his hand and profess my undying affection. The feeling, though, was a start.

I was about to respond to his "sometimes" comment when I caught sight of a familiar face and turned to watch Mitch Palmer escort a women to a table on the beach. She had high cheekbones, skin the color of dark maple syrup and a dancer's grace, her hair and shoulders moving in slow rhythm with her hips.

Old Eagle Eye noticed almost as quickly as I had. "You know those two?"

"Mitchell Palmer, son of Charles Palmer, the attorney and wealth manager. When he isn't representing crooks, he's golfing with the mayor. I don't recognize the woman."

"Tamika Williams."

She wore a summer dress of swirling color, split to mid-thigh, and cork espadrilles that accented the definition in her legs.

I stared. "Who is Tamika Williams, besides gorgeous?"

My tone sounded sharp and I couldn't see Tony's reaction but, judging from the mirth in his voice, he was having fun at my expense.

"She works in the city planning department."

Mitch guided his date into a chair. With a hand deftly gathering the dress, she slid onto the seat as if gravity didn't apply.

"How do you know her?" I asked.

"I've seen her around the station. She knows somebody in Patrol."

Her fingernails were a long, dusky red. As she fluffed her napkin and scanned the menu, I felt a hot flash of jealousy. Mitch and I had dated a few times, and I thought we'd clicked. But after I chased down Junior in a yacht owned by Mitch's father, the relationship went south. Maybe because I'd wrecked the boat and papa had declared me persona non grata. Or maybe because I'd been obsessed with solving other people's problems instead of my own.

It shouldn't have mattered. I now had a chance to connect with a man of greater stature and maturity, someone who was as handsome as he was athletic, and far more tolerant of my moods than anyone other than Walter. But watching Mitch dote on Tamika, I felt bereft. In Tony, I'd finally gotten what I wanted, only to discover that maybe I didn't want what I had, only what I didn't.

We concentrated on the food. The waitress refilled our glasses. I passed on dessert, my mind drifting toward the music of my childhood, Alan Jackson singing about how he'd try to love only one, his voice cutting through me like a steak knife.

After teasing the diners for an eternity, the sun bade us farewell with a wink and slid beneath the water. The entire restaurant, including the bartender and wait staff, erupted into applause.

I couldn't clap.

8.

THE NEXT MORNING, I found Cheryl on the first floor of InSpire, her eyes skimming the welter of agents, politicians and media that crowded the lobby. There were a lot of them, browsing the pastries while awaiting the big reveal.

Without turning her head she said, "You look like hell."

"Hello to you, too."

The leather crackled as she rested her arms on her utility belt. "How'd the date go with the lieutenant?"

"It went."

Her back to the corner for the best vantage, her head seemed in constant motion. "No wonder you look beat. What happened, or shouldn't I ask."

"Please don't."

The lobby offered a grand view of construction on the second of the InSpire towers and the hole that Rae and I had punched in the window of the first. Police tape crossed it like the ribbons service families tied around trees. Despite the city's frenetic growth, this remained Spanish Point's newest high-rise. The iconic wedge of glass and steel had just opened when one of my fellow agents was murdered in the penthouse eighteen floors above. It felt wrong to stand below and celebrate the construction of anything involving leisure, yet it was our job. I hadn't been consulted about the venue.

Cheryl's voice cut through my thoughts. "You OK?"

"I was thinking," I said, glad that someone cared enough to ask, "that all the money in the world can't erase what happened here."

"Amen to that."

Cheryl turned her head toward the elevators. I followed. Three people looking crisp and coifed approached the podium. My new employer, Casey Laine, assumed a position in front of a half-dozen TV screens that showed renderings of the proposed complex on the bay. Even in her power suit, Casey looked thin and pale, with penciled eyes and a trapdoor mouth. Flanking her was a tanned and suited Tommy Thompson, lead developer of the project and husband of the late Susan Thompson. And last but not least, Casey's soon-to-be-former husband, Mayor Phil Cunningham, athletic in a bespoke suit the color of a silver ingot. Thompson helped my boss onto the platform with a solid hand to the middle of her back. Cunningham caught the gesture and frowned.

Cheryl clacked her gum. "I bet those two are going at it like rabbits."

"Let's give the rabbits some credit."

I wasn't in the mood for gossip, or pomp, let alone a rematch with hizzoner. On the plus side, this would be one of his last official acts before ascending to the statehouse in what looked like a rout of his opponent, an environmentalist who'd made the mistake of criticizing the economic lifeblood of the area, the building trades.

Laine appeared beneficent, tenting her hands as if in prayer, a smile moving the spiky bang that overshadowed her forehead. The consummate host, she would MC the show. But it was the city's gig, and the politicians weren't about to be upstaged. They had contributed a fair number of lawmakers, aides and officials to the mix. But Casey had seen this rodeo before and packed the crowd with at least fifty of her agents and supporters, who threaded among the audience with elastic smiles and copies of the presentation.

Casey's daughter, Melissa Cunningham, followed the pack, distributing pens that were branded with the Laine & Company logo of an antique schooner and yellow index cards on which we were told to write our questions. Normally, Melissa was styling. She had clothes by Dolce and breasts by Mattel. Today she resembled a fashion model, undernourished and glum. While her mother shouted her power in shocking red, Melissa had chosen a dress of black lace. Unsteady on a pair of strappy heels, she passed without comment to stand, head bowed, beside her mother.

Cheryl fed a piece of gum into her maw. "She looks like somebody killed her puppy."

"That's harsh," I said.

"You should be happy somebody looks worse than you."

The first time I'd spoken to Melissa, she'd appeared at a similar presentation with Mitch Palmer on her arm, lips and nails the color of dried blood. Nervous and courteous to a fault, Mitch had assured me there was no relationship, that he was merely escorting the daughter of a client. Our subsequent dates had proven his claim. Despite Cheryl's invitation to bash a potential rival, seeing Melissa suffer did nothing to lift my mood.

At the sound of a thumping mic, I looked toward the podium to catch the interplay between Casey and her husband. While she launched into a spirited description of the project, knowing all of us shared in the excitement of any groundbreaking for vertical construction, the mayor folded his arms and tapped the floor with a polished shoe, an impatient actor waiting for his cue.

After Casey's introduction, Thompson fielded the microphone and remote, fanning through slides with gestures that resembled a Hail Mary pass. For Spanish Point, the concept seemed ambitious. Where InSpire would provide more housing, the new project was, in essence, a thirty-four acre park bordered by a canal with docks, a new arts hall and a row of mixed-use residential, commercial, entertainment and office properties. The design offered unobstructed access to the bay, with the city's signature Baywalk promenade encircling the site like a ribbon.

The project seemed a better use of public land than surface parking. It was democratic, too, providing access to the water for people who couldn't afford the million-plus price tag for a room with a view. My biggest worry concerned the removal of the riprap seawall. It was the only barrier protecting the site and a significant part of the downtown from flooding.

Paying for all this was the big question, one that Cunningham addressed. Philanthropy would fund the design, public and private money the construction, with operating capital courtesy of user fees and tourism tax—an example of the partnerships his administration had championed.

I knew what was next. Cunningham couldn't let a moment pass without reminding residents that this great city would be even greater if reactionary forces weren't holding it back. "It's time," he said, "we stop striving for mediocrity."

On that cue, Thompson returned to the podium for the grand revelation. Suitcoat abandoned, tie loosened and striped shirt cuffed to the elbows, he announced that, as with the DeSoto Park project, Laine & Company would serve as the exclusive seller's and rental agent for all retail, food service and housing on the site.

That triggered a gust of applause from the agents, but not as much as the final slide, the unveiling of the name and the branding campaign to accompany it. The city and the developer had haggled for months over names like Bayfront, Bayside, even Marina Plaza, though the project lay a good mile-and-a-half north of the docks where Walter Bishop and others anchored their boats. With a trumpet volley from the sound system, Thompson announced that the new project would be called Vertex by the Bay.

"Vertex?" Cheryl shouted above the noise. "What kind of name is that?"

"I think it means pinnacle," I said, joining in the applause so I didn't look like a spoilsport.

"Sounds like vertigo."

"Wait until you see the prices."

As we filed from the lobby, Melissa distributed the official press release. I folded it into a pocket and didn't stop until we'd reassembled on the patio behind the performing arts center, with a clear view of the breakwater that protected the city. The heat had started to pile up. Shading my eyes, I turned to ask Cheryl if the cops had nailed the thugs who'd trashed the Kawasaki when a crew from the Gulf Coast News Network dumped its equipment next to us and a short blonde with a thousand watt smile extended a hand.

"CW," she said in a throaty voice that had earned a boatload of awards. "We meet again."

I'd encountered Leslie Ann Roberts three years ago when she'd covered the kidnapping of my grandfather. Unfortunately, age had only tempered that professional mask with a sensual flair, her hair spilling over dark brows to highlight the smooth skin, straight nose, full lips and smoky eyes that could start a riot.

To deflect my jealousy, I introduced her to Cheryl.

Reaching across to shake hands, Roberts squared her body as if ready to pounce. "I hear you've landed the big one."

"You mean a job with Laine & Company?"

"I mean the Incredible Hunk, Tony Delgado."

I'd seen Roberts as a rival for Tony's affections while we'd hunted the kidnapper. Tony had become the de facto spokesperson for the department, a role he seemed to enjoy. So did Roberts, who beamed a little brighter whenever she interviewed him. I'd considered her an aggressive talking head, a reporter with more interest in advancing her career than uncovering the truth. As the investigation progressed, I discovered an unsettling truth of my own: that, with her mix of insight and compassion, she was often better than me, or the cops, at asking questions.

I trained my eyes on the far side of the patio, where the dignitaries had donned white hardhats in preparation for the groundbreaking ceremony, and scratched my face.

"Sorry to hear about the accident," she said. "If that's what it was."

Had Casey not leveled me with the evil eye, I might have shared some of the details.

Roberts intervened. "I completely understand. My husband spilled his Harley last spring."

Two years ago, she'd married the station's weather guy, breaking the hearts of her male viewers.

"Sorry to hear." I met the sparkling eyes. "I'll bet that's the last time he rode anything other than a lawnmower."

She chuckled, a sound that fit the ear like music. "No more boy toys."

I nodded toward a bulldozer perched at the water's edge. "Tell that to the politicians."

Hardhats in place, the dignitaries stumbled toward the bay, Casey deftly picking her way over gravel and grass. Roberts excused herself and, barking something to her camerawoman, followed.

We watched her walk, hips rounding as smoothly as pistons.

"That was close," I said.

Cheryl nodded toward a group of protesters milling across the Trail. "You guys aren't home yet."

I couldn't read the signs but knew they would condense massive health and safety issues into a few catchy phrases. It was possible the crowd also included wealthy condo owners who stood to lose their water views once Vertex went vertical. A very democratic mix.

Street noise wouldn't normally carry this far west, but the marchers were blasting rap music and the volume was starting to irritate the pols. Several tapped their smartphones and within minutes a pair of officers herded the pickets onto the sidewalk. The music had a solid beat. It wasn't country, but I would have swayed to it if Casey hadn't caught my eye from her perch on the shoreline. Maybe she worried I'd join the march.

Shrugging, I focused on the real star of the show—the bulldozer. A hardhat who looked as if he actually worked in construction helped Cunningham aboard and started the machine. With the television camera rolling, the mayor lowered the blade and ran the dozer into the riprap. Casey had told us the bulldozer symbolized how Vertex would provide access to the bay for all of the city's residents. It was good theater, until the blade jammed under the coral and the machine bucked, threatening to topple the mayor into the drink. Leaping onto the dozer, the hardhat saved the day, and the dignity of the mayor, who dismounted with a wave to his fans.

I would have enjoyed the scene more if a woman had captained the construction equipment, but this wasn't a venue for equality, social or financial. The agency would make some money, so why fight city hall? We were all smiles. It could have been civic pride, or the thought of the commission on a six-million-dollar condo overlooking the Intracoastal, given the median price of a home in the county clocked in at two-forty and change.

Casey stepped to a microphone set between a pair of speakers and, in a clear voice that competed with the pickets across the street, touted the benefits of progress. Her conclusion was a classic. With Vertex, she said, Spanish Point had finally earned the distinction as a luxury destination. At that pronouncement, the protesters increased the volume.

Cheryl leaned into my ear. "This," she said, "is gonna start a frickin' war."

9.

WE SKIRTED THE pickets, hiking the block-and-a-half to the new offices of Laine & Company, a gaggle of agents fluttering like gulls over scraps at the beach. Judging from the random conversations, we were excited about Vertex, concealed weapons and the propriety of wearing sunhats while showing a property, roughly in that order.

The new office occupied a third of the block on one of the most trafficked intersections in Spanish Point. The building consisted of a gleaming two stories of cantilevered steel and glass. High-brow, Walter would have called it. It reminded me of an aquarium with a cleaning service. Casey had asked for a contemporary version of mid-century modern. She'd told the local newspaper that, for our clients, the glass would lower the barrier to entry. For her agents, it would bring the outside in, a celebration of our place in the sun. Judging from the lack of walls between the desks, the building was the physical equivalent of Facebook. Only in the placement of the restrooms did designers consider privacy. They'd painted those walls purple.

As we reached the traffic circle that formed the main intersection in town, Melissa drifted like a dark cloud, falling in line as we filed past a model of a two-masted 19th Century schooner that had appeared overnight.

I pointed at the ship. "When did this happen?"

"Over the weekend," Melissa said.

In contrast to the pristine glass, the ship appeared out of time and place, its wood darkened with moisture, the sails as brown as parchment and equally unprepared for a storm.

"Why?" I asked.

"Mom says it symbolizes the agency and crew," she said in a singsong voice. "Everyone pulling in the same direction."

"I think she's confused us with galley slaves."

We entered the building and its cooling wave of air, past images of showcase properties printed directly on the glass. I said hello to the receptionist. Ignoring her, Melissa clacked across the tile to her station outside her mother's office. My desk faced three others. Leaning back in a chair that resembled a black sieve on wheels, I blew out some air and considered my options. I could search for Walter and those assholes who hit Rae and me. Or I could earn a living.

I decided on the latter. After signing onto the computer network, I worked my rather sparse contact list to produce listings, and to nudge a couple of fence-sitters into closing. Every few minutes I'd glance over my shoulder to see if anyone was listening. Apparently not. Most were too busy forcing cheer with their clients. It sounded like phone sex.

As the office cleared—agents didn't make a lot of money sitting at their desks—I began calling marinas I'd skipped the first time to ask if anyone had spotted the *Mary Beth*. No joy, as the British liked to say. I felt depressed. Given the office obsession with productivity, there was no way I could visit those places in person without running afoul of Casey.

In my detective days, I'd found that, if I was jammed for ideas, focusing on something unrelated often yielded results. So I found an article from the *Harvard Business Review* on the open-office concept. I'd seen the piece on my phone but wanted a deeper dive, not that I'd ever bring it to Casey's attention. She believed a workplace designed without doors would encourage employees to communicate face-to-face.

The research showed the opposite. People in open offices isolated themselves. They tuned out noise with headphones. They made sure others wouldn't overhear their conversations by sending email and texts. They looked busy, which always scores points in an industry all about curb appeal.

I switched to the agency's website when Melissa approached. With her heavy-duty eyeshadow and liner, she resembled a sleep-deprived raccoon. Stopping at my desk, she clutched her shoulders, the blood-red nail extensions digging into her arms, and produced a soulful look.

"Mom wants to see you in her office." She appeared to shiver.

Mom had the same effect on me. "At least we're doing this in person."

For a moment she looked puzzled, then the air went out of her like a discarded pool float. "I know this sounds bitchy, and I should have told you earlier, but you look like you did a face plant on a waffle iron."

"And you look like you're under arrest. Is everything OK?"

"You should go see Mom before she gets really pissed."

* * *

Casey Laine's office looked as spare as its owner—glass on three sides with a wall of windows in back. No filing cabinets, credenza, artwork or flowers. From her bio I knew she'd come up old school, fighting harder than her male colleagues for a shot at her own brokerage. The décor said she'd not only made it but wasn't going to yield to anyone, especially a man. Maybe that's why eighty percent of her agents were women. That, or we were more empathetic when dealing with clients. Face-to-face, as it were.

She sat behind a desk consisting of a single sheet of glass on transparent legs. There were four items on top—an inbox, an outbox, a transparent cup of pens and an 8x10 of Melissa taken during her college days. The photos she'd kept in the old office of Phil—the triptych showing him while golfing, fishing and driving—was gone.

Casey had shed the power jacket to display a candy-stripe blouse in blue with the sleeves cuffed to her forearms, a mirror image of Tommy Thompson. Despite the breeze near the shore, her spiky hair had managed to stay in place.

I congratulated her on the presentation. With the barest nod, she thanked me. I asked if she knew what was bothering Melissa. "I know it's not protocol," I said, "but I'm concerned." If her demeanor to this point had been cool, the look she returned dropped a few degrees. Even with the strong backlight, I watched a blue vein ticking at her temple.

"I noticed you were talking with that reporter from Gulf Coast News."

"Leslie Roberts," I said.

"What did she want?"

"Her husband dumped his Harley last spring and she was commiserating."

"You know only Melissa and I can speak for the agency."

"Understood," I said, hoping an air of contrition might lead us to the real issue.

"We're not here to discuss boats or motorcycles." She smiled like a halibut on ice.

"No, ma'am." I resisted the urge to genuflect.

"I'd like you to review the agency's code of conduct. We have certain expectations of our crew members. I know you're still caring for your grandfather, but please limit those visits to your own time, as well as anything involving the police—unless it's an official summons. In that case, we'll transfer your duties to another agent. No more running off unannounced. As long as you're working from this office, please post your schedule with Melissa. Put in the required desk time and continue to do your follow-up calls and we should get along fine."

Calling on my training as a police officer, the first rule of which was never aggravate your superior, I gave her a curt "Yes, ma'am" and the now practiced look of obedience—the brief nod and compression of the lips I'd adopted in Pennsylvania for my watch commander, a horse of a man who thought a woman's place was in the sack, not behind a badge.

"Good. I'm glad that's settled. Now." She rifled through a stack of papers and handed one to me—although knowing Casey's filing system, this was yet another performance designed to humble the newbie. "This is the inventory and price list for the remaining units of InSpire One and presale prices for the second tower. Square footage and amenities are posted on the website. This," she extracted another paper and passed it across the desk in a crisp move, "is the presale list for the first of the Vertex towers. We've negotiated the same arrangement with Tommy Thompson as we did with InSpire: the more units an agent sells, the greater the commission."

The papers were Excel spreadsheets with great detail and incredibly small print. I wondered how Casey read them without her half-frames.

"You're sure you're up to this." It was a statement, not a question, carrying with it an element of dismissal. "I thought you looked a little askance during the presentation."

I made a mental note to control my facial expressions. "Everything's fine."

"I trust you're being honest. I understand you have some doubts about opening the bay to redevelopment."

"Not doubts. Just a few questions."

Her eyebrows, plucked to uniform arcs, rose a millimeter. "Such as?"

"Is it cost-effective to place our most expensive real estate in a flood zone?"

"You would be the first to admit that we cannot deny landowners the rightful use of their property, as long as that use is consistent with the law."

"Aren't we putting those residents at risk?"

"That's the buyer's decision, although I can see why you'd come to that conclusion."

It was my turn to raise the brows.

"Coming from law enforcement, as you have."

I produced a weak smile. "The problem isn't people making their own decisions. It's governments writing policy that encourages those risks."

She folded her arms in a defensive gesture. "Lulling them, as it were, into a false sense of security."

I nodded.

"And who is responsible for that?"

"In this case," I said, "the city leadership."

"By leadership you mean my soon-to-be-former husband."

"As I said, I'm just asking questions, not assigning blame."

The air streaming through her pinched nostrils sounded like my grandmother's steam iron.

"I know you take it as a personal failing that you could not save Susan Thompson, but we need to move on."

Not true. My failing was in not nailing Phil Cunningham for her murder. She'd been pregnant. It took no great leap of logic to infer that the mayor's lover was bearing the mayor's child. She'd been shot on her return to town from the airport during one of his political rallies. At the time, I'd done more than express my doubts, after which hizzoner had filed for a temporary injunction to prevent me from confronting him. The ploy had worked.

Casey was still speaking. "You've expressed doubts about Phil's involvement in her death. I don't need to tell you that suppositions like that are dangerous. As I said before, I will take care of our family's business. You take care of yours, which is selling the Gulf Coast. I hope you can find the time to do that."

"Yes, ma'am."

"I know your heart is in the right place, Candace, but we don't think with our hearts."

I bristled. No one except my grandparents was allowed to use my first name. From a back pocket I pulled my phone, checked the time and said, as sweetly as possible, "If you'll excuse me, I have a showing at three."

As much as I disliked a berating by Laine, I wasn't looking forward to the tour. It involved Mitch, of all people, acting on behalf of a friend, a euphemism if ever I heard one. *Chin up,* I thought as the agency's air conditioning swept me out the door. *At least you get to meet the competition.*

10.

THE COURTYARD OF The Palms on Main had every amenity a single working person could imagine. In its courtyard, the kidney-shaped pool gleamed, trees shaded the chairs and sun umbrellas sprouted like mushrooms. A tiki bar provided rapid relief from dehydration after a long day in the water. Through the pergola, a trail led to a dog park with a fire hydrant. There was even a cart that sold sunscreen and shirts.

Surrounding it were six stories of alternating cream and yellow stucco, overlooking the play yard from windows and balconies that seemed to smile. And why not? The Palms provided an upscale oasis for the upwardly mobile, with perks and prestige to suit.

The luxury did little to reassure me. I had envisioned today's tour with Mitch Palmer's new inamorata as a showdown, the female version of *mano a mano*. But instead of fireworks, I was getting fizzle. Dressed in a clinging wine-colored wrap and sandals Cleopatra might have admired, Tamika Williams looked less like an office drone than a starlet at the Academy Awards. Touring the courtyard, she catalogued each amenity, tucking her chin and widening her eyes for emphasis while punctuating her praise with oohs and aahs. At times her face shown with a childlike wonder, the same expression that must have graced mine when I walked through my first mansion on Spanish Key.

Money will do that, especially when you don't have enough.

Had the day started as usual, I might have felt more charitable. But brushing my hair had sent a shower of glass shards bouncing into the sink. My arms burned, my leg throbbed and my face resembled a tire tread. No amount of concealer would cover the scrapes. And the itching. . . .

Then there was the interminable groundbreaking and Casey's pious lecture, all running interference with today's schedule. And even though the drive from the office to The Palms measured less than a mile, traffic had turned the roads into sheets of corrugated metal, baked by an unrelenting sun.

So I was in a questionable mood when I arrived at The Palms, a place that straddled the gentrified part of the city between the downtown and its sketchy neighbor to the north. For a working girl, it was Tamika's best bet. Despite our agency's full-court press, I couldn't show InSpire, or even hint at Vertex. Every unit there topped three million plus a hefty maintenance fee. She could never afford that on a city worker's pay, so I'd swung the SUV toward the edge of the downtown and hoped for the best.

The tour had started well, Mitch and Tamika expressing condolences about the motorcycle accident while saving their enthusiasm for the property. But as we entered the complex, the light on her face dimmed. Smart and professional in her designer dress, shades and smartwatch, she couldn't hide her dismay. As we passed the row of amenities — the bar and coffee shop, library, game room, fitness center, store and branch bank — it must have occurred to her that someone had to pay for all this. And, as a renter, that someone would be her.

Mitch Palmer, late twenties with an athlete's body and a quiff of hair sprouting from his forehead, seemed unmoved. He stood at attention by the elevator and avoided eye contact with me, his jaw as tight as the pant legs of his suit.

"What do you think, T?" he asked as he held the elevator door.

He would have a pet name for her. At any moment, she'd break into a song from *West Side Story*.

"It's lovely," she said, and kept her own counsel until the doors closed.

But in response to an icebreaker question about what had brought her to Spanish Point, Tamika started to talk. Her family came to this coast from Jacksonville. Her father worked in trucking and her mother cleaned rooms at an assisted-living facility. I also discovered that she wasn't a lowly clerk but the city's lead planner.

"She's the one who greenlighted the DeSoto Park and Vertex projects," Mitch said with the pride of a parent at high school graduation.

T. corrected him. "I recommended them for approval."

The elevator doors opened onto a glassy corridor and the apartment door opened onto a foyer flanked by bedrooms in a split plan design, with living, dining and kitchen areas straight ahead. Everything had a contemporary look. The plank tile resembled barn board, the chandeliers clusters of grapes, the floor lamps wheels of cheese. The kitchen continued the post-industrial theme with white cabinets, black appliances and chrome stools. The capstone was a balcony that afforded a direct view of a condo tower that offered a direct view of the bay. It was the thought that counted.

As she glided from feature to feature, Tamika wind-milled her arms, a look of awe and joy flushing her face. She'd grown up humble and I was betting this was the closest to lux she could get. Despite her gyrations, the place looked out of reach. Unless someone came to the rescue. On that point I felt torn.

Mitch had picked up the scent. Hands in his pockets, he reminded T. to budget for living expenses as well as the rent.

Her face, when she turned, had taken on the look of a question mark. That was my cue. I gave her the snapshot: rents ranged from $1,200 a month for a 572-square-foot studio to $2,800 a month for this 1,400-square-foot unit. Furnished apartments topped three grand. An earlier check of my smartphone had pegged the average salary of urban planner at $44,176 a year. The rent on a one-bedroom unit would run almost twenty thousand a year, more than half of her take-home pay. No wonder young people fled the area. They couldn't afford to live here.

Tamika absorbed the information, squeezed her watch and suggested we move on to the next property. Avoiding eye contact, Mitch and I agreed. I'd return the keys and meet them there.

* * *

On the short trip across town—an excruciating ride that required sitting at red lights for a week—I got to hear Randy Houser belt out a full-throated version of "How Country Feels." The singer was making me homesick. I stopped play and felt some relief as I glided into a neighborhood shaded by mature oaks.

Compared with The Palms, the Spanish Bay Apartments looked sedate. An older complex, its adobe arches and wrought-iron rails overlooked a narrow ribbon of greenspace. There was no pool, café or dog park. What the apartments offered was character, and a laid-back vibe. It was Tamika's idea to focus on housing close to city hall. Admiring the human scale of the place, I was developing a grudging respect.

"Now this," she said as we cleared the mullioned door of a two-story unit, "is old school."

It was old, I'd give her that. The fit and finish wasn't lux— Formica covered the counters, an air conditioner jutted from the window and a plastic shower curtain encircled the tub. The place could have used some updating, but with its arched doorways, hardwood floors and screen door to admit fresh air, the apartment was livable, if not a classic.

The effect wasn't lost on Tamika. The more she looked, the more animated she became, describing to Mitch what she could do with the place, her head cocked, hands splayed or rolling in a fluid motion.

"And," she said, "I can walk to work—as long as I carry an umbrella."

We discussed price. She could rent a two-bedroom interior unit for $1,300 a month or an end unit with six extra windows for the same price. She wanted the corner apartment—a good choice, I agreed, and promised to deliver the paperwork by midweek.

Pinching the sides of her smartwatch, presumably to read the time, she apologized for skipping the third showing but said she was on an extended lunch hour and had to return to work. She offered Mitch a ride. He said he'd walk to his office.

"So what was going on back there?" I asked as Tamika's car rounded the corner.

He stood tall and serene in a blazing dress shirt and tie, his suit jacket draped over a shoulder in a practiced move. The midday sun highlighted the stubble on his chin, no doubt his idea of rebellion against corporate life.

As if pulled by a powerful magnet, he turned his head but kept his body pointed toward the office. "What do you mean?"

"You hardly said a word in there, or at The Palms."

"There's not much to say."

"It's like you're here but still avoiding me."

"I like the hair. The streaks. You've got that Jennifer Lawrence, Kate Beckinsale thing going on."

"Highlights," I said. "Are you and Tamika serious?"

He shrugged.

"Have you told her about us?"

"What's to tell?"

He'd spoken the truth and the truth hurt. We'd dated briefly and spent a passionate night in his condo on the beach. But after I wrecked his father's yacht, expensive even for a wealth manager, we'd drifted apart.

Mitch had eyes the pale blue of periwinkle. They locked on my face as if looking through to the other side. "Tough luck about the accident. You all right?"

The rapid change of subject jarred but I found the attention touching "I'm able to sit up and take nourishment, thanks for asking, but it's been a lot worse for Ryan Donovan."

"The kid who drowned at the jetty."

"He was the nephew of a friend." I sketched the story. At my request, the police hadn't released my name, saying only that the body had been discovered by a bystander. With Casey looking for any excuse to thrash me, I didn't need the publicity. I asked him to keep that knowledge to himself.

He nodded and checked his phone.

"You're never this quiet."

"Sorry." He slid the device into a pocket. "It's this Vertex deal. Stocks, bonds, VC money. Public, private. It's a monster. Lots of players, lots of moving parts. I feel like I'm juggling cats."

"I hear the taxpayers could be on the hook for the whole thing." I didn't share that I'd heard the rumor from a ride share jockey I barely knew. At this point, details like that didn't seem important.

"We're solid," he said, angling his body toward his office as if reconsidering an escape. "The city floats the bonds and TPI offers stock to raise capital."

"TPI?"

Thompson Partners Inc. You didn't read the release?"

I hadn't but kept that to myself. "Isn't this what you financial types call a *moral hazard*? Using public money to encourage people to take more risk than they normally would?"

He shifted the suit jacket to the other shoulder. "The city blessed the issue. Moody's rated it A1, Standard & Poor's and Fitch A plus. It's a good allocation of capital."

"No offense, but if you apply enough grease, the politicians will approve anything."

"These doubts wouldn't have anything to do with the mayor, would they?"

I could feel the censure coming and decided to steer the conversation to a less volatile topic. "Tamika seems nice. Where did you two meet?"

"At the gym."

"She doesn't look like she needs it."

His eyes made the full circuit of my body. "If it wasn't completely inappropriate in the Me Too age, I'd say neither do you."

I felt like saying that falling off a motorcycle kept me trim. Instead, I thanked him and wished them both the best. Tamika was lovely. Why take out my frustration on her? And what had Mitch done to me? Listened to my doubts about out-of-control growth? Loaned me a boat? Offered a relationship when I wasn't ready?

Watching Mitch disappear around a corner, I compared him with Tony. They were both decent, one young and active, the other established and mature. Mitch raised my blood pressure. Tony raised my IQ. Amazingly tolerant, he even pretended to like country music. Then why wasn't I full of sweetness and light? Did I want Mitch because I didn't have him, or couldn't?

And then there was Tamika, confident, competent, a public servant who didn't have a father rolling in cash. Could she even afford this place, unless she and Mitch were planning to live together? In which case I felt more miserable than before, which I didn't think possible.

Somedays I hated this job.

11.

DESPITE THE PROMISE to focus my energies on work, I had a duty to find Walter. And the best place to start was with Lois Danforth.

That was harder than it sounded. Last month I'd taken her dog, Sugar Bear, after Lois had threatened to abandon the animal. The dog was sweet. I hadn't been. The crisis started when I'd wondered whether Lois was a good fit for Walter, after she'd asked him to relinquish the sailboat and his black lab for a life of Stepford houses and manicured lawns. Walter disagreed, I overreacted and next thing I knew, he'd hoisted anchor and, racing ahead of the second hurricane of the season, sailed the *Mary Beth* to parts unknown. That was three weeks ago, and no one I knew had heard from him since.

Lois's house looked different. It wasn't just the storm shutters that covered the windows and half of the front doors. It was the trash—rows of boxes neatly stacked on the grassy fringe between sidewalk and street.

By the time I parked and walked to the door, sweat had dampened my back and palms. I punched the bell and listened to it echo, hoping, though I'd called ahead, that Lois wasn't home. She answered in the same outfit she'd worn when sailing with Walter, a nautical-striped top and capris with strappy sandals in gold. She looked high-tone and fresh, a contrast to her last appearance, when she'd mourned the loss of her sister with vanquished eyes and a bottle of red.

The living room appeared as antiseptic as it had on the last visit, which was to be expected from a retired ER nurse. There was one exception. In addition to leather furniture floating in a sea of white tile, Lois had lined a wall with boxes, their computer-generated labels bearing the names of various destinations—kitchen, living room, den, basement, garage.

Inviting me with a restrained wave to sit, she asked if I wanted iced tea and returned with two glasses garnished with lemon wedges. She placed the glasses on coasters depicting the Spanish Point marina. I took the recliner. She took the couch.

I could see what had attracted Walter. She had a slender nose, expansive eyes and blonde hair with more layers than a wedding cake. She also had a regal reserve that spoke of inner strength. The definition of polite, she crossed her legs, folded her hands and, ignoring the scratches on my face, asked what she could do for me.

I opened my mouth to inquire about the boxes when she blurted, "It's about the dog, isn't it? How is she? I've been worried about her."

"She's with my neighbor and her daughter. They're good people, and the dog has room to run. But that's not why I came. I first wanted to apologize for the way I behaved the last time I was here, for the questions I raised about you and Walter. And for stealing your dog."

She touched the corner of her eye, something I'd done many times with mine to keep the lid from twitching. "There's no need to apologize. I couldn't take care of her. The dog kept staring at the lake, and you know our HOA won't allow anything off a leash." She tented her fingers, tipped with frosted pink nails, over her heart. "And I wasn't the most gracious host."

"That's understandable. Your sister had just died." Susan Thompson, intimate and victim of the lord mayor.

Lois sipped tea and stared into another room as if looking back in time.

I asked, "How are you holding up?"

"It's interesting how time passes, how it seems to rub the edges off your grief." She moved her hands as if applying lotion. "But there are times when I feel guilty, as if it were my responsibility to protect her. I think you know what that's like."

I did, and wondered if Walter had told her how my father had returned home one night and killed my mother and brother in a house fire. It wasn't a story I liked to share, but there it was.

I pointed the conversation in another direction. "I'm sorry."

"Sorry for what?"

"For not having Phil Cunningham charged with your sister's murder."

She traced the rim of her glass, something Tony had done at the restaurant. "You will."

"We have no evidence."

"I have faith in you."

"I wish I did."

"Ask Walter when he returns. I'm sure he'll help."

My expression must have given something away.

"I know what you're thinking," she said. "'If he returns.' If this is anyone's fault, it's mine. I shouldn't have insisted he move in with me. To give up his dog, his boat, the life he'd built after the loss of his wife. . . ."

Walter's wife had died of cancer—she was the Mary Beth after which his sailboat was named. And while he was fond of Lois, I knew he didn't want to relive the emotional turmoil of love and loss.

"Have you heard anything?" I asked.

"No, nothing. Except for the postcard."

I straightened. "The postcard?"

Rising, she disappeared into the kitchen to return with the mail. "This came a few days after Walter left."

The postcard showed the golden sails of the Sunshine Skyway Bridge. On the other side, Walter had written Lois's address and a two-word message: don't worry. The card had been postmarked nearly three weeks ago, the day after Walter disappeared. It had been mailed from St. Pete, a whopping forty miles north of Spanish

Point. I'd called all over the state and never considered that the boat could be that close.

The postmark answered the question of where he'd been. Walter could have berthed the *Mary Beth* and mailed the card on the way to one of the airports. The bigger question was why. An experienced sailor, he could easily outrun a storm. Unless the storm had damaged the boat, why had he hauled anchor only a few miles from Spanish Point? And where had he gone from there?

I thanked Lois for the tea and the loan of the postcard and, on my way out, pointed to the stack along the wall. "I know this should be obvious, but what's with all the boxes?"

"I'm returning to Connecticut. All of my family is there, or what's left of them." She did a good job of covering the hitch in her voice.

"Then Walter doesn't know you're leaving."

She shook her head. "He came by to put up the storm shutters. At that point, I wasn't sure where either of us was going."

The boxes reminded me of the forts I'd built with my brother Colton. Our protection from the outside world. It hadn't worked for us; I doubted it would work for Lois.

"When do you leave?" I asked.

"The movers come on Monday."

I had a week to find Walter. If I convinced him to return, he'd have a chance to say goodbye to Lois. And, if he felt he couldn't stay, he could say goodbye to me as well, the last of his extended family.

It was a chance I'd never had.

12.

"CHERYL," I YELLED at the phone as it bounced on the seat of the SUV, the truck crawling past the used car lots that cluttered this section of the road. I'd have preferred to ride the Kawasaki but it remained in the garage, the bike only slightly more battered than me.

I was heading north to St. Petersburg, less than an hour's commute from Spanish Point, with no plan other than to search every marina I could find. Cheryl was my ace, when we could hear each other. Bluetooth wasn't working to connect the phone to the SUV's dash and she kept yelling at me to speak louder.

I did. "Does Walter have any buddies who own a marina around Tampa Bay?"

"What about that deputy he used to have coffee with?"

"Which one?"

"You're gonna love this."

I braked for another of the endless traffic lights and watched the phone sail onto the floor. "Cheryl?"

The tinny voice arose from the floor mat. "Ray Parrish."

"You're kidding. The deputy who served me with the restraining order?"

"Insult to injury," Cheryl said. "Fate moves in mysterious ways."

"You mean Phil Cunningham moves in mysterious ways." Cunningham was the one who'd applied for the restraining order.

"You beat it, right?"

"At great peril to my reputation."

"Reputation." She snorted. "Listen to her. You want the address or not?"

"I hang on your every word."

She gave me the address. "And don't get chippy."

"I didn't know you followed hockey."

"I can't hear a damned word you're saying," she said and the phone cut out.

* * *

The last time I'd seen Raymond Parrish, the Palmetto County Sheriff's deputy had had the nerve to serve me on the *Mary Beth*. Even in his body armor, his uniform of dark green and gold couldn't hide a belly that spoke of too much time behind a desk. Today, dressed in a Sheriff's Activities League T-shirt and baggy cargo shorts, he looked less voluminous. He still sported a horseshoe of hair rimming a tanned scalp, a gray mustache that could have doubled as a paintbrush and a grin halfway between lecherous and wry.

I'd managed to fish the phone off the floor and call ahead. He hadn't rejoiced at the call but agreed to meet. Greeting me with a handshake that was remarkably dry, given the humidity at the edge of the harbor, he invited me inside. He said nothing about the motorcycle accident.

The office consisted of a wooden desk in the corner of a cavernous metal building northerners would call a pole barn. The building housed rows of boats in various states of repair. It smelled of metal shavings and industrial-strength glue. In the middle stood a lathe that slowly turned a mast. Stepping over a puddle of what looked like oil, Parrish hit a red button dangling from a cord in the rafters and the machine ground to a halt. He wasn't wearing safety goggles or earplugs. Tough guy.

Once in his lair, his bearing changed. Giving me a stare that embodied a suspicion of everything in the world, he asked what had brought me to these parts.

I surveyed the shop and its dry-docked fleet. "What exactly do you do here?"

"Why don't I give you the tour?"

At this rate, the trip would take most of the day, which meant I'd miss the staff meeting at work and any chance of selling condos at InSpire. Or ingratiating myself with the boss.

We walked the inside perimeter of the building, Parrish pointing to rows of fishing and motorboats hoisted on a grid of girders, the craft in storage while their owners summered in Michigan and Maine. The boats came in three sizes—big, bigger and biggest. I'd never understood why people poured so much time and money into these things. Maybe instead of real estate I should sell watercraft. They were certainly popular.

Parrish must have felt uncomfortable with the silence. That or he was anxious to return to work, because he paused near a tangle of drill presses and saws and asked me what I wanted.

I took the direct route. "I'm looking for the *Mary Beth*."

"She's here, safe and sound, or will be, when we're done with her."

The "we" seemed an exaggeration, since Parrish and I were the only two people in the place.

"What happened to her?"

"The jib tore in the storm. Walter was afraid he'd lose it, and the mainsail."

"I thought trying to outrun a hurricane was a rookie mistake," I said. "What was he doing out there in the first place?"

"You'd have to ask him."

"I'd like to. Where can I find him?"

Parrish folded his arms across a barrel of a chest, a classic sign of shutdown. "I couldn't say."

The blood rose to my neck like a heat rash. I tried to keep the anger from my voice. "Do you know when he's coming back?"

"No idea. He just said to have her ready by the first of the month."

"It's a little past that."

He grinned. "These things take time."

"And you don't know where he's gone."

"Walter doesn't confide in the help."

"Seriously, he didn't leave a forwarding address, or say when he'd pick up his boat?"

Parrish shook his head.

"And you're not worried about getting paid?"

"With Walter? I thought you said you knew him."

I thought I did, too, but this disappearing act made me question that assumption.

"Where was he heading? Tampa, St. Pete, the airport?"

"He said he might visit some friends."

"Which friends? Where?"

Parrish shrugged and angled his body away from me, another sign he wanted to end the talk.

I handed him the postcard Walter had sent to Lois. "What do you know about this?"

He flipped it, read the back and returned the card. "It's a postcard."

"From this marina. There's a rack of them twenty yards from your door."

"They're for tourists."

"I bet you gave him the stamp."

His mouth twitched.

"Come on, deputy. What's with the spy stuff?"

"He knew you'd trace the boat. He just wanted to slow your progress a bit."

"You mean you want to slow my progress. That's why you agreed to meet, and offered the tour, and won't tell me if the boat is even here."

Parrish shrugged. "What can I say?

I struggled to lower my voice. "You're sure you don't know where he went."

He raised a palm. "I swear on my sacred honor as a law enforcement officer, I have no knowledge of his whereabouts."

The man was yanking my chain and enjoying it.

Parrish started toward the door, a sure sign my time had expired. I tried a different approach. "Can you at least tell me where Louie is?"

"He's resting comfortably at home."

Of course. Walter would occasionally use Parrish as a kennel when he worked extended shifts with his security service.

We'd come full circle to the battered wooden desk. On it sat a pile of work orders and a set of keys. I recognized the AA medallion. Out of options, I asked Parrish if I could see the boat. Maybe there was something Walter had left behind to indicate where he'd gone, and why.

Parrish said he couldn't allow that. "Maybe you two are friends, but I need permission."

"And, with Walter missing, there is no way to get that permission."

"Who said he's missing?" The twitching lips broadened into a grin and, gesturing toward the brilliant square of light at the end of the building, he headed toward the entrance. The second he turned, I pocketed the keys and rejoined Parrish on his stroll, lengthening my stride to make him work to keep pace. Height had its advantages.

We moved outside, the sunlight toasting my hair. At this rate, I wouldn't need to add highlights.

Parrish and I shook hands. I thanked him for his help and headed toward the parking lot, away from the marina. Once I was sure he'd gone inside, I doubled back and, starting to the south and moving in a clockwise direction, I combed each dock until I reached the middle of the pier. The *Mary Beth* was moored at Dock C, Slip 32, buried in a clutter of boats. Walter had furled the mainsail and the jib was gone. There was nothing above deck except the helm and a boom pointing at the wind like an accusing finger.

Checking for prying eyes, I stepped aboard, unlocked the hatch and climbed belowdecks, scrabbling down the narrow stairs to feel my way to the utility drawer where I knew Walter kept a flashlight.

Gripping its rubberized base, I played it over the galley before heading along the narrow corridor to the stateroom.

It was darker here, with curtains drawn over the portholes. Walter had built a nightstand into the wall near the bed. I opened the only drawer and began pawing through a stack of papers, setting them on the mattress in two piles, one for nautical maps and tools of the trade, the other for anything personal.

A folder caught my eye. In it, Walter had accumulated a number of newspaper clippings, crisp and brown, dating to 1991. With a sinking heart I read about the fire that had taken my family, and the speculation as to why my father had set it. The bigger question was why had Walter saved these stories? By my calculations, he'd have been about twenty-five at the time of the fire, a young state police officer assigned to help the fire marshal investigate a double homicide.

At the bottom of the drawer, Walter had stowed what looked like a slim yearbook, with group shots and individual portraits of the state police officers in his barrack. Several of the troopers had written inscriptions beneath their photos, congratulating Walter on various milestones during his time of service. Maybe Walter had stayed in contact. It was worth a shot.

A phone check of the internet yielded Northeast Pennsylvania addresses and phone numbers for three of the troopers. Propping the flashlight on the nightstand, I called the first number. A recording told me it was no longer in service. The second rang forever with no pickup. After an interminable series of rings, the third call connected. An elderly woman answered with a muffled hello.

"Mrs. Keen?" I asked. "Is your husband there?"

"He's in the garden. Who shall I say is calling?"

It was a bit late in the year for gardening but I identified myself and said I was calling about Walter Bishop.

The received clunked. I heard her voice, a faint reply, the sound of doors slapping and metal clanking, and then the bark of a voice.

"Sergeant Keen?" I asked and repeated the introduction.

"I know who you are."

I wondered why but stuck to the topic. I said we feared Walter's boat had swamped in the hurricane and wondered if he'd gone north.

"You just missed him."

"What was he doing there, if I might ask?"

"You'll have to ask him."

Years in law enforcement had taught me to expect the answer. It still angered me.

"Where can I find him?"

"I'm sorry, I can't help," he said and hung up.

The boat suddenly pitched to starboard and footsteps thudded on deck. I managed to stow the book and clippings and reach the galley as sunlight burst through the hatch.

13.

"I'M BANNED FROM the marina," I told Cheryl as I jogged to the truck.

"What'd you do now, wreck another yacht?"

"B&E." I swung the SUV into traffic, my ear glued to the phone. It still wouldn't connect to the dash. At this point, I didn't care if I got a ticket for failing to use a hand's-free device. "I entered private property without the permission of the owner." I made air quotes around "private property," which Cheryl couldn't see.

"Tell me you weren't charged."

"I left without a stain on my character. And, get this, I found Walter's boat."

I sketched the details. Former Deputy Raymond Parrish hadn't seemed alarmed to see me rise from the hold like the Phoenix. In fact, he'd smirked. I'd changed that expression. Shoving the keys and a business card into his chest with enough force to make him totter, I said if he heard anything from Walter I'd better be the first person he called. I had a good six inches and twenty years on Parrish and, gray hair or not, I'd dropkick his butt into the harbor if he held out again.

"He's a nasty SOB," Cheryl said. "There's gonna be payback."

"Not after OSHA gets done. I reported him for operating a hazardous workplace without proper safety gear."

The phone beeped. I told Cheryl I had another call.

"Don't put me on hold!" she yelled.

I did. The second call came from the garage. The Kawasaki was ready for pickup. That created a problem: I couldn't drive both vehicles at the same time.

Cheryl had disconnected. I swung the SUV onto the interstate and hit redial.

"You are a piece of work," she said. "Why are you chasing this guy all over the Gulf Coast?"

"Walter? I miss him."

"Gotta be more than that."

"He's my ballast. He keeps me from obsessing and doing really stupid things."

She clacked her gum. "Then tell him to get back here fast."

"Your confidence is touching."

"You called for a reason," she asked, "or to waste police time?"

"I just got off the phone with the garage."

Her radio squawked. "Gotta go. Duty calls."

"Wait. Don't hang up."

"Some of us have to earn a living."

"I need a ride to get the bike."

"What do I look like, a taxi?"

I thought about answering but she'd disconnected.

* * *

Given the location of the boat, and the postmark on the card, the logical airports for Walter to fly from were Tampa or St. Pete. When I got to the office, I'd check the direct flights—he hated layovers— and go through the motions of canvassing the ticket counters. If Melissa didn't overhear and report me to her mother, who'd haul me in for another lecture. Or worse.

For now, there was little I could do. In a few hours, I had one of those make-or-break showings, another two-million-and-change condo on Spanish Key. It was fairly lowbrow for the barrier islands but, if the deal closed, I could get the Kawasaki out of hock. That meant dropping the SUV at home and calling Gary Hudson. He'd given me his direct contact information along with another sales pitch about his value as a CI.

Once more unto the breach.

* * *

Ten minutes later, Hud's bright red Prius lurched to the curb. Given the congestion, I couldn't understand how he got anywhere so fast. Once again, he pried himself from the car and, like a climber seeking handholds, maneuvered across the side of the car. Hand raised as if to strong arm him, I said we could dispense with chivalry and managed to open the door by myself.

Two bottles of water sat in the cup holder in front with another two in back. He'd also laid in a supply of peanuts in those small bags used for airline snacks.

"You're well-provisioned," I said.

"All I need now is a hot dish."

"Hot dish?"

"It's Midwest for casserole."

"We're not going there today."

He took a deep draft from one of the bottles and adjusted the rearview mirror, most likely to get a better view of his passenger. "Where to?"

Holding the phone I said, "I texted, remember?"

"I watch *Taxi*, the TV show, you know? The one with Louie and Alex and the Reverend Jim. I had dreams about hailing a cab and Marilu Henner drives up and says, 'Where to, big boy?'"

"Too much information," I said, confirming the address of the garage and suggesting he head north on the Trail so I could check the progress of InSpire Two.

Winking as if we were conspirators, he put the car in gear and drove, the radio ablaze with Tim McGraw's "I Like It, I Love It."

I dispensed with the preliminaries. "You said you had information about Ryan Donovan. I understand he worked for an engineering firm doing a geotechnical survey for Vertex."

"The company's a division of Fox Construction, the people doing drainage work on the keys."

"What do you know about Ryan?"

"He got fired for reporting a problem to city hall."

That confirmed what Rae had said but didn't add anything useful. "What problem?"

"The numbers. They didn't add up. I hear the kid was sharp, figured out somebody was fudging the tests. They must have found pockets in the limestone or something. This strip here, along the Trail? It's like the San Andreas Fault for sinkholes."

We passed a dozen communities with gatehouses and monuments engraved with names like Sherwood Forest and the Hamptons before entering the commercial strip and its collection of medical buildings, paint stores and sports bars.

"Can't the builder compensate for that?" I asked.

"How? They can't pop a high-rise on a place that floods every time it rains. The limestone gets honeycombed with caverns—the water eats away the rock and leaves gaps. It's like the way caves are made. Here's what I hear happened. The kid finds evidence of these pockets in the raw data but not in the final report. He knows the holes lead to subsidence, so he alerts his boss. The boss doesn't want to hear about it. Next thing he knows, the city OKs the project. The kid has a conscience. He goes over his boss's head and tells some guy in Thompson's development company about the report. You know about TPI, if you're selling his condos, you're working for them. When nothing happens, the kid tells somebody in city hall and the next thing he knows, he's fired. They called it insubordination. I call it a cover-up."

"And then he drowns," I said.

He blew through a yellow light. On Sunday, he'd driven as if he were asleep. Today he was auditioning for NASCAR. With Hud, there was no middle ground.

"Go figure," he said.

"That's what I'm trying to do. Can you slow down a little? This isn't a race."

"Time is money." He glanced in the rearview mirror and winked.

"What do you hear about the drowning?"

"That a very high personage was with him."

"High personage?"

"The daughter of your boss."

"Where did you hear that?"

"I know the guard who runs the gatehouse at their development. Fellow Navy guy. Straight-arrow, takes exception to being bossed by the upper crust. Says it reminds him of 'Nam."

"You think Melissa had a hand in Ryan's death?"

"Something was going on at the house that night, a party, maybe, or somebody over for dinner. Melissa calls down to the gatehouse and says to let this Donovan kid in. He's driving a Subaru Outback with a board strapped to the top. Car goes in, then nothing. Shift changes, it's getting light, and out comes the Soob, flying like a bat out of hell. A couple minute later, he's followed by a black Beemer, driving so fast it nearly clips the gate arm."

I recognized the car. "Melissa?"

"At this point, the guard doesn't know. He calls the house to make sure they haven't been robbed."

"Is that normal?" I asked, knowing that, in the rarefied world of the keys, it probably was.

"They're like rock stars out there, and they tip big at Christmas. The guards keep an eye on them."

"Who answered the phone?"

"Nobody. Usually, it's the mom picks up. So the guard checks the barcode records and finds out the daughter drove home that night but the mom didn't."

"So Melissa was alone with her boyfriend and they had a fight."

"You're missing the big picture."

"Of course," I said.

"Nobody knows where Melissa or her mother were when the kid drowned."

"And you base that theory on your source at guardhouse."

"I volunteer with the police. Copying, filing, directing traffic during the parades—the grunt work they don't wanna do. You'd be amazed at what cops say when they think you're not listening. It's like being a candy-striper at the hospital. At first, they look at you cross-eyed but after a while, you just blend into the walls, you know, the guy limping around on crutches, doesn't understand ten codes, what's he gonna do. You want, I could keep my ears open. Go undercover, be your silent partner."

We'd reached the sharp bend in the road just south of the marina and DeSoto Park and would soon pass the towers before heading east toward the industrial outskirts of the city. Even if he hadn't pulled the case, I had to call Tony, just not from the car. For now, I found myself growing impatient. I didn't want a confidential informant. And I didn't want a date. I just wanted a ride.

"Gary," I said.

"Hud."

"Hud, I'm no longer a cop."

"You still need the 4-1-1, right?"

"Even if I were in uniform, I'd have to abide by Rachel's Law."

His eyes scanned the road. "Never heard of it."

"It requires the police to provide guidance for the safety of their informants."

"I'm just saying I could help."

"And I wouldn't go around offering that service to any of your fares. If you're not trained for the work, it's dangerous."

He squirmed, a reaction, I thought, to the rejection of his offer.

"You OK?" I asked.

"Gotta make a pit stop."

"I'm sure there's a bathroom at the garage."

"I'm diabetic. I have to eat at certain times and drink a lot of fluids. You got some good info today for the price of a ride." He tapped the water bottle on his forehead. "I think a reward is in order."

I watched traffic thicken and strip malls crowd the road. "I've never paid a source."

"I don't mean money, although I hear you real estate agents make a pretty penny."

"I hate to sound insensitive, but what do you want? And if you say a date, I'm getting out right here."

That brought another chuckle. "How about you buy me a pop?"

"Is that Midwestern for soda?"

"Diet, only thing I drink besides water. There's a convenience store at the next stoplight."

I knew the place. The cops called it the Stab 'n' Grab. Cheryl had been heading there the night she stiffed me on a ride from the hospital. A stop would delay my reunion with the bike but a drink was a small price to pay for Hud's cooperation, so as he coasted into the parking lot I agreed.

"Do you always leave the car running?" I asked as we stepped onto the broiling asphalt.

He used a metal crutch to point to his leg. "The AC helps."

The demonstration focused attention on my own leg, which complained every time I bent it. "What if someone else needs the AC?"

"Who's gonna steal a Prius?"

I offered a hand but he powered in a zigzag crouch toward the door. As I held it open, I spotted two people wearing hoodies. They paced near the counter, their bodies twitching as if plugged into a wall socket. My skin wanted to crawl.

"Hud?" I reached for his arm but he'd already pushed inside.

14.

THE TALLER OF the two figures flipped through gum and candy bars at the counter while the shorter one jittered near a rack of Little Debbie snacks. Males, judging from body size and shape, dressed for stealth, not heat. They wore black jeans and black-and-white high-tops. One sweatshirt featured faded pentangles, the other an image of Jerry Garcia with a Santa hat. Heads down, they scanned the store. The clerk, a middle-aged woman with a headscarf, noticed them, too, because she lifted a cell phone to her ear.

The air seemed to stop moving. Then Hud ambled from the restroom and, propping his crutches against the drinks station, started filling a foot-high cup with a brown slurry. Before I could reach him, the guy at the counter showed a gun. The clerk froze, her face a knot of fear. The taller of the two barked something. Dropping her phone, the clerk scooped cash from the drawer and extended her hands as if making an offering, the loose coins pinging across the counter.

As the men turned, I got a full view of their faces. It was the pair from the bar, down to the tattoos and piercings. Bottlenose didn't appear armed but Skulls waved the weapon as he hustled toward the door. I felt more than saw Hud move and tried to block him with an arm, but he shifted right, drew a pistol from his cargo shorts and, braced against the counter, leveled the gun.

"Hold it!" he yelled.

Bottlenose blinked. Skulls took aim. Grabbing Hud by the shirt, I yanked him below a shelf as the gunman opened fire. We hit the floor hard, glass from the fluorescent tubes spattering our heads. Ears ringing, I rose as the pair banged through the door in a dash across the lot. Praying they weren't on foot, I followed. They dove into a late model Jeep with black wheel rims and a tow winch and, squealing across the asphalt, hooked a left and raced toward the Trail.

There was no time to ask for permission. With a quick checking to ensure that Hud and the clerk were OK, I ran for the Prius and floored it, reaching the highway in time to watch the Jeep speed south. Hugging the curve past the botanical garden, I raced the car through red lights, the traffic parting like the Red Sea. When we hit a straight stretch, I managed to pry the cell from my pocket and call 9-1-1, throwing the phone onto the seat with the hope that Dispatch could still hear me.

We roared past the villages of Osprey and Nokomis, the Jeep whipping from lane to lane to maintain its lead. Despite the open connection to the emergency center, with no scanner, radio or backup, I was flying blind, and we'd reached a critical spot near the cutoff to the city of Venice. If the Jeep headed straight, the police chopper could easily track it. If the pair veered onto the island, I could jam them in the congestion. All bets were off if they turned left and headed for the mostly undeveloped land east of the interstate.

They hit the bypass and took a sharp left, crossing three lanes of traffic to race past a shopping plaza and two retirement homes. A mile later we hit a traffic circle, the Prius pulling G's until I thought my brain would leak, before we flew under the interstate and into the wilds.

"Where the hell are the cops?" I shouted at the phone as the road narrowed and the scrub pressed close. And where were these guys going? This was Venice, a community where people watched Lawrence Welk every afternoon at four. Aside from the terrorists who'd trained for the 9/11 attacks, it was the last place on earth anyone would expect a pair of thugs to hide.

With the commercial strip behind, the buildings thinned. Finally, as the Jeep hit a straight stretch, a squad car screamed past, siren and lights blazing. I moved the Prius onto the grass but kept rolling as another cruiser flew by, both too busy to bust me for speeding. We took more turns, the roads shrinking, sidewalks and streetlights giving way to a dense scrub of palmetto. I followed the pack to a crossroads, took a left on what felt like two wheels, then another and finally ran the Prius across a bank near a stucco house with an overgrown lawn, the Jeep parked sideways in the driveway with the squad cars blocking its exit.

Positioned behind their cruisers, the cops broke out body armor and shotguns and, after what seemed like a lengthy exchange with Dispatch, circled the house. In the distance, sirens flared. Overhead, a flapping noise caught my ear as Air One, the sheriff's helicopter, came in low above the tree line.

Reinforcement arrived, cars with badges from three police departments and the sheriff's office. A mobile command center rumbled in front of the Prius, as did an ambulance and a pumper from Fire/Rescue. Deputies took the lead, using a bullhorn to address the pair inside the house. There was no reply. The deputies tried again. Still no response.

A crowd of neighbors gathered at the corner and I joined them, asking if they knew who lived in the house. One of the women said the owner had died. They thought his grandsons were staying there now. Nobody liked them, or their friends. Too much noise and traffic at night.

Arms extended in a shoving motion, an officer waved us back. We'd moved to the neighbor's mailbox when the front window shattered and bullets ripped through the trees. Yelling for them to stay low, I pushed two of the women into the grass. We waited, surrounded by the rattle of engines and the stink of diesel. Head raised, I watched as a contingent of deputies in olive battle gear hunkered behind cars and the command center. To their credit, they hadn't returned fire.

A young officer crab-walked along the line of cars to our position and, face like a bad sunburn, yelled at us to return to our homes and stay there. I wasn't about to be driven off before the cops breached the building, so I led the neighbors along the street before doubling back to settle behind the Prius. The car afforded cover, and a clear line of sight to the command center, where a plainclothes cop stared at the house, a cell phone pinned to his ear. From his intense expression, I assumed he was negotiating with the pair.

Voices barked from radios. Someone used the ten code for backup, ETA less than a minute. Training their weapons over the hoods of the patrol cars, the officers settled down to wait. When the SWAT team arrived, it unloaded a robot used for defusing bombs.

Not a good sign.

The robot resembled a silver box on wheels, two feet by three feet, with a camera on one side and a claw for grabbing explosives. Deputies outfitted the claw with something that looked like a flare and maneuvered the robot to the side of the house without windows.

The plainclothes officer traded his cell for a bullhorn and told the fugitives this was their last chance to surrender. He got no response. Wobbling on clunky wheels, the robot climbed the slope and, extending its claw, pressed the package against the masonry. Someone yelled, an explosion tore the air and, as smoke covered the yard, the SWAT team poured through the hole. As the dust drifted, the team hauled a man from the house, planted his face on the lawn and cuffed him. Turning his head, his lips buckled against the ground, his arms a dark stain of skulls.

"Where's the second guy?" I said to myself and started when someone answered.

"What guy?"

Cheryl stood behind, hand on her weapon. With all the commotion, I hadn't noticed the patrol car. Or the TV news van that sat behind her cruiser.

I pointed to the SWAT team as they bundled their prisoner into a blue-and-white. "They're the guys, the ones who hit Rae and me."

"Dispatch said some woman called it in and chased them all the way from town."

My heart hammered. "They would have escaped."

"You're becoming a real menace."

"Don't you have someone to arrest?"

"Once a LEO, always a LEO—unlike your buddy."

In the confusion, I'd forgotten about Hud. "Is he all right?"

"Last I heard, but we'll have to cite him."

"For what?" I asked. "Trying to save a life?"

"For carrying concealed without a license."

I took a beat. "No good deed goes unpunished."

"The law's the law. We just enforce it."

"See what you can do for him, OK?"

"Why? He the new boyfriend?"

The light had shifted. Even with sunglasses I had to shade my eyes. "At least he offered a ride when I needed one."

She hooked a thumb over her shoulder. "Speaking of rides, you might want to take a hike before the press finds you."

"You afraid I'll get the credit?"

"More likely the blame."

"Why?" I asked. "It's not as if shots were fired."

Cheryl tipped her chin toward the SWAT vehicles as they lumbered down the street. "Won't matter. Someone in their infinite wisdom is gonna claim excessive force."

Heart firmly back in my chest, I took a breath. "I'm a little rusty on protocol."

"Stop by later and I'll give you a refresher."

15.

FROM THE CONCRETE pad in front of Cheryl's house, I rang the doorbell, knocked and, when no one answered, stuck my head in the door and said "hello" in my best imitation of Martha Stewart.

Cheryl wasn't in the kitchen and Tracy must have been in the back of the house doing homework, so it was up to Sugar Bear to greet me. At least that's the story my goddaughter told as she bounded from her room with a big smile and a hug to match.

I bent to nuzzle the animal, a pit bull rescue with a white diamond on her neck and a lopsided head that looked as if she were asking a question. "How is she? Have you been taking her for walks?"

Tracy was still in her school uniform of white blouse and tartan skirt. She beamed. "After every meal."

"Sounds like brushing our teeth," I said.

She was a skinny third-grader with Cheryl's deep eyes, narrow face and flyaway hair. So far, she hadn't discovered her mother's cosmetics. Cocking her head, she stared at me.

"What happened to your face?"

"Aunt Candace had an accident."

"Aunt Candace is an accident," Cheryl said as she pulled a T-shirt over her head.

Tracy scampered toward her bedroom, Sugar Bear trotting after.

"How's she doing?" I asked.

"The dog? Fine, no thanks to you, dumping that mutt on us."

I detected the trace of a smile. "I did not dump. Tracy welcomed her with open arms."

"Twisted arms, is more like it."

"She's a rescue dog," I said. "She needs a good home."

"You need a good home."

"She's cute."

"So's that lump on your forehead. Keep it up, I'll give you another one to match."

"My, we're surly tonight.'

She led the way to the kitchen where she ferociously chopped carrots while two big fans on poles scattered her hair. A pot on the stove ticked and the oven emitted the crisp smell of bread. Cheryl was making spaghetti, the only meal the woman knew how to cook, not that I wasn't grateful for the invitation to dinner. I used to cook for two, before Pap went into assisted living.

"You'd be surly if you let one of the bombers get away."

"Who got away? The guys in Venice?"

"Don't you ever watch the news? We're getting pasted."

"Timeout," I said. "The SWAT team arrested both of them."

"One of them."

I felt gut-punched. "How? I was standing right there."

"Did you see 'em bag the second guy?"

I shook my head.

"That's because he slipped out before we secured the perimeter."

"Bottlenose?"

"The guy with the metal in his face."

"Shit."

"Use your inside voice."

Tracy bounded into the kitchen with Sugar Bear close behind. Grabbing a handful of silverware, Cheryl told her daughter to set the table and feed the dog. I watched her work.

"You don't think Tracy knows what you do?"

"I want her to feel safe."

"Then don't send her to school."

"That's funny. You come over to mooch another meal or did you have something constructive to say?"

"Go back to the two guys I chased. Who are they?"

Cheryl poured two glasses of iced tea, handed one to me and tipped her head toward the back door. "A couple of beauties."

She led us onto a small patio with uneven pavers and a rusted table that sprouted an umbrella. The table rocked when we sat. Water still covered half of the yard, same as mine next door. We'd called the county but there wasn't much they could do. The massive influx of people had led to the construction of acres of nonporous surfaces. High tide caused storm drains to surge. There wasn't any place for the water to go.

Luckily, Cheryl didn't mention my part in selling serenity by the square foot. Instead, she rattled off the names of the men, confirming what the neighbors had said, that they were living with the grandfather. She recited the arrest report from memory. Most was boilerplate. My ears perked when she got to the weapons cache the police had seized. A search of the home had yielded 112 firearms, ranging from an AK-47 and AR-15 with a grenade launcher to a large capacity shotgun, an MP28 Schmeisser and a .45 caliber Thompson submachine gun. Police found silencers, gas masks, practice hand grenades and materials for making explosives, as well as methamphetamine, cocaine and marijuana.

"Jesus," I said. "What were they doing, going to war?"

"We're looking at their Facebook page now. It's the usual sovereign citizen crap."

"What I'd like to know is why they rammed the bike."

"And didn't smoke you with an RPG?"

I gave her a grim smile. "You think the mayor sent them, like those bikers he sicced on me during the tourist murders?"

Cheryl chewed ice.

"It's a working theory," I said.

"Nobody works it but you."

"They're his mules, I know it." But even as the words tumbled out, I had doubts. The guys I chased were too old for Cunningham's charity, too random, too petty in their anger. If Mayor Phil had wanted me dead, I'd be dead. The man didn't take prisoners. Apparently, neither did the bombers.

"It's simple," Cheryl said. "You cut 'em off in the parking lot and they ran you down."

I drained my glass and watched the condensation puddle on the tabletop. "What were they thinking?"

"I don't know. That the two of you were lesbians?"

"Jesus."

"That's what the older one's got tattooed across his chest."

"He should have inscribed the Ten Commandments."

"No room."

Rising, Cheryl collected the glasses and opened the door with her foot. "Give it a rest. You keep talking like this, you're gonna bring the whole city down around our ears."

"I let them get away."

"Only one of them." With an elbow she shut the door and headed for the kitchen, where she told me to grab some bowls and fill them with lettuce. "Don't beat yourself up. You did good. Hand me the celery."

"I stumbled on them. It was an accident."

"You gave us an ID, and hung in there 'til the cavalry arrived."

"They could have blown up the entire block."

"Welcome to paradise, home of terrorists, assassins and red tide. This isn't a sleepy little fishing village anymore."

"Duly noted."

Cheryl tossed spaghetti into the water, set a timer and stuck her head around the corner. "Dinner!" Tracy and Sugar Bear trotted into the dining room. We carried salad and cruets of oil and vinegar to the table, said grace and ate. The timer sounded. Cheryl rose to plate the dinner, adding a gravy boat of sauce and a platter of rolls to the table.

I helped myself to a small portion of pasta. "Speaking of reports, what's the word on Rae's nephew?"

Cheryl winced. To Tracy she said, "Close your ears."

Her daughter giggled and snuck a piece of roll under the table.

"Blunt force trauma to the head. Don't feed the dog. You'll make her sick."

I gave Tracy a wink. "The ME's sure?"

"The rocks did a number on him. No way to figure out if he'd been hit before going into the water. But I will tell you this: the kid had more confidence than smarts."

"So we're ruling it an accident."

She took a mouthful of spaghetti. "We. Listen to you."

"What about Walter," I said. "Any word?"

"Who do I look like, Allan Pinkerton?"

Sugar Bear ate another piece of roll. Cheryl gave Tracy the cop stare. The girl asked to be excused and skipped to her room. We cleared the table, washed the dishes and adjourned to her front stoop to watch the rainwater drag palm fronds along the gutter.

Cheryl offered a piece of gum. "Now what."

"We find out what Ryan knew and who he told."

"How, pray tell, are you going to do that?"

I folded the gum under my tongue. "Talk to someone who was there."

"Who?"

"You remember Dean Caldwell, the contractor?"

"The guy who looks like James Caan? Walter's buddy?"

"Two birds," I said.

16.

THE BAY LOOKED beautiful at this time of day, cupping the city like a smile. The air had cooled to the low seventies, a light wind blowing from the east, the humidity dipping as we headed into the dry season. A motorboat skimmed the Intracoastal. A flock of white ibis foraged its rim. A peace in contrast with the events of the week..

Standing in DeSoto Park not far from the spot where the Jeep had hit my bike, I watched the light, strong and direct, gild the skyline, the windows of InSpire reflecting the morning in a kaleidoscope of color—blue sky, marshmallow clouds, the watercolor green of the banyan trees.

Across the inlet, the skeleton of the second tower stretched as if roused from sleep. Cranes hefted beams, buckets poured cement and workers crawled scaffolding sandwiched between floors. They were marvels of engineering, these towers, glass wedges as sleek as fish, modern versions of the spires that graced the Pennsylvania countryside where I once lived. In the clean light, the built environment looked as beautiful as the natural one.

Pap's illness had brought me to these shores, but it was days like this, scenes like this, that had convinced me to stay.

Less than two months to go before the end of hurricane season and, so far, we'd had no repeat of the back-to-back storms that had flooded the park. With a deep breath I dispatched a thank-you for calmer weather and, hoping that calm would extend to my personal issues, headed toward a white construction trailer hunkered at the building's base.

Dean Caldwell was in his office—the great outdoors. Tall and broad in the chest and shoulders, he'd dressed for work in khakis, blue Oxford and white hardhat. As usual, his clothing looked spotless, something I didn't think possible in the construction trade. He stood between two workers while holding what looked like blueprints over a makeshift table of plywood and saw horses.

Dean managed one of Tommy Thompson's companies, Fox Construction, running the crews that were building InSpire and Vertex. A friend of Walter's, he'd helped me track the scum who'd kidnapped my grandfather. When we'd met, his company had been installing drainage systems at Spanish Key Beach. A short time later, he'd discovered a body in one of the box culverts. Nothing like a murder to seal a friendship.

Looking across the park, he waved and, dismissing the workers, greeted me with a warm smile and an iron grip.

"Well," he said, removing sunglasses to reveal a pair of frost-blue eyes. "Look what the cat dragged in."

"I know."

"What happened to your face?"

"I fell off the apple cart."

"You mean you upset the apple cart, or fell off the turnip truck?"

"A bit of both." Hooking a thumb toward the police tape that encircled the first tower, I told him about the motorcycle crash. He crossed his arms and pushed out his lower lip, disapproval and sympathy in one move. No wonder I liked him.

"You're a day early," he said. "Where's the boss?"

I assumed he was referring to Casey and our planned tour. I said we'd see him at the open house but that today I'd come on a mission for a friend.

"Which friend?"

"Rae Donovan. The Fox division doing site-prep for Vertex—her nephew worked for them."

"What's his name?"

"Ryan Donovan." I sketched the details, from Ryan's dismissal to his drowning.

"I did read about that. Didn't the police rule it an accident?"

"That's what we assumed, until we heard about the report that Ryan flagged. I'm just wondering if there's a connection."

"What report?"

"He believed the tests showed that water had undermined the limestone beneath the project, but the report to city hall omitted that data."

"That," he said, "is a serious charge."

I saw a smaller version of myself reflected in his sunglasses. "It could be a serious problem."

"I think better on my feet," he said and escorted me around the perimeter of the building.

The construction crews had finished four of the eighteen floors and were starting on the fifth. We skirted the outer fence with its green visual barrier and had to raise our voices to hear above the clank of rebar and slurry of concrete.

As we neared the bay, Dean slowed his pace. "What's your interest in this, other than your friend?" His voice held a touch of frost.

"If I'm going to sell these condos, I wanted to make sure the owners are safe. How would we know if there is subsidence?"

"Ground subsidence is the same as sinkholes." He pointed north. "There are none, or your car would have disappeared on your way in here."

"But if there was something. . . ."

"The tests would show it, and since they didn't. . . ." He let the sentence hang.

"But if there was something, how would it show up?"

"You mean here?" He jabbed a thumb at the tower. "You'd see cracks in the concrete. Spalling. Rust from rebar."

On the fifth floor, a worker balanced on a grid of two-by-fours that hovered over the edge. "You guys are busy. How would anyone notice?"

He cleared his throat. "We do a visual inspection. Every day."

We walked the northern leg heading east, the peaceful park clashing with the scramble of voices, the ping of metal and rush of concrete. "Can you get a copy of the report?"

"You can get it at city hall."

"I mean the original."

Turning the corner, we found ourselves back at the makeshift table. "There is no original. The company fired this guy for cause. End of story."

He'd landed a sucker punch, and even though I should have known it was coming, it still hurt. "So you knew about this."

He surveyed the park and the street beyond, the main artery through town growing thick with traffic. There were no protesters today. "You can't start a rumor like that."

"What if it's not a rumor?"

He lifted his sunglasses and I felt the terrible weight of his eyes. "There's a lot at stake here. A lot of money, a lot of jobs."

I tried to lighten my voice. "Come on, Dean. You know I'm going to harass you until you spill."

"What does Walter say about this?"

"He's missing. But you knew that."

He refitted his glasses, and whatever connection we'd had vanished.

"You could do a visual inspection of both towers."

He raised a hand the size of a mallet. "If word gets out, work stops on Two." He jabbed a finger at Tower One. "Even if we find nothing, those people panic and the first person they call is their lawyer. The city pulls the permits for Vertex. Thompson stock craters. You've got millions in delays and legal fees, all because some kid wanted to be a hero."

"So you can't do it."

"On a hunch?"

"What if Walter were here?"

"He's not."

Another sucker punch. "You know something I don't?"

He crossed his arms. This time the gesture wasn't endearing. "I have no idea what you know."

Deep breath time. "OK," I said. "Thanks for your time."

He gave me his back. "Don't mention it."

17.

CHAOS REIGNED AT city hall. Usually, it confined itself to the inside. Today it cluttered the entrance and spilled out.

Moving their traveling show from the bay, the Vertex protesters had reconvened at the west-side entrance to the building. There were about fifty of them, shading their eyes or ducking under trees. They surrounded a sculpture consisting of cantilevered layers of slate, an installation not unlike the condos of DeSoto Park. Atop the artwork stood a lone woman, small of stature and loud of voice. Dee Hansen, one of the city's five commissioners and a rival candidate to Cunningham for a seat at the statehouse, was giving a speech.

Hansen was well-known in local politics, a tireless advocate for balanced development, which made her the odds-on favorite to lose the election. Two years ago, insiders had written her off as a fringe candidate. But since her near-death experience in the car the night someone had shot and killed Susan Thompson, Hansen had become a vigorous defender of Florida's natural environment.

With the doors to the east entrance cordoned for repairs, I'd paused to plot the most direct route through the crowd, giving me a chance to watch Hansen in full flight. She was impressive, even if I did sell real estate for a living. She prowled, she gestured, she called her audience to arms. With her frizzy hair and pinwheel arms, she resembled a minor prophet without the beard.

Voice coarsened by an inadequate PA system, she reviewed the results of studies on climate change, published over the summer by the local newspaper.

"The mid-range projections by NOAA show the seas around our state rising up to twelve-and-a-half inches by the year 2030. Those scientists predict extreme high tides will occur sixty percent more often this year than in the year 2000. Higher seas will push seawater inland. It will flood neighborhoods, kill vegetation and pollute our drinking water supplies."

She blamed global warming and the industrial interests who caused it. Most of the crowd applauded, except for the guy on my left, a clean shaven, middle-aged man with a coal shovel jaw. He'd remained silent during the bit about higher seas but the reference to industry apparently pushed his buttons.

"Global warming's a hoax," he yelled. "The seas have been rising for thousands of years."

To my rear, a voice called my name—a short bark I instantly recognized. I withdrew from the crowd.

"You join the enemy now?" Cheryl asked.

"I'm meeting someone. What are you doing here?"

"Keeping the peace."

Hansen and the heckler were now talking over each other.

"Good luck with that," I said.

Hansen abandoned statistics for examples. "Miami Beach is already responding to sunny day flooding. They're spending millions of dollars raising roads and sidewalks and replacing their drainage systems."

"Miami was built on a swamp," the man yelled. "Which is where all of you belong."

"That's enough for me," I said and asked Cheryl if she knew of another way into the building.

"Watch and learn," she said. With a hand securing her service weapon, she excused herself and pushed through the crowd.

Inside the building, I lifted my face to the cooling flood of air conditioning and asked Cheryl what I should do about Caldwell and his hidden threat.

"Nothing hidden about it," she said as we ran the gamut of onlookers, workers and visitors clogging the entrance. "You trash his company, he loses his job, maybe his retirement. You might as well have threatened his wife and kids."

"I didn't see a wedding ring."

"Maybe he thinks you were making a play for him."

"I did *not* make a play for him. Where do you come up with these things? Is Tracy reading *Cosmo*?"

She smacked her gum. "That's not even close to being funny."

"It's just that I considered Dean a friend, or at least a friend of a friend."

"Burned another bridge, did we?"

We'd reached the center of the building and a wall that showed a timeline of the county's history. A large television was tuned to CNBC. I grabbed Cheryl's arm. Charles Palmer and Mayor Cunningham were speaking remotely from Spanish Point. They stood on the slight rise of ground that would become the amphitheater for Vertex, the text of their conversation jittering across the screen. In the background, white sails skimmed the bay while the condos of Spanish Key rode the horizon like stacks of thousand-dollar bills.

Palmer dressed in a blue pinstripe suit with a plain red tie, Cunningham in a summer-weight sports coat and open collar, sandy hair matching his boyish smile. The man was nothing if not telegenic. They were talking about the city's recovery from the recession with someone in the studio, who kept referring to the pair's frequent appearances on the show. So when it came, the question was a softball. Palmer's answer straight from the PR playbook.

"I would consider this the greatest boom in the city's history since John Ringling brought the circus to town," he said.

The mayor echoed Palmer's endorsement with his metric of progress. "It's great to see the skyline filled with cranes."

The pair smiled while the interviewer repeated their names and thanked them for the insight.

"Caldwell thinks Thompson's stock might tank," I said. "Watching those guys, I doubt there's a chance of that."

"That should make your job easy."

She was right, of course. Heading for the elevators, I raised a bigger issue. "Tell me I'm doing the right thing."

"Tell me what the hell you're doing."

"I'm calling on Tamika Williams to deliver the rental agreement. If she has time, I'd like to talk to her about Ryan's death, and how it might relate to the geotech report, which may or may not be a forgery."

"Maybe you should go to the company first."

"They ignored Ryan," I said.

"Then talk to your boss."

"Do you think she'll listen if it means pulling the plug on the biggest score of her life?"

"You know Thompson. Talk to him."

"I've only met him at social functions."

"So you're gonna do what the kid did and go over their heads."

"Rae deserves an answer."

"You always had a soft spot for family and friends."

"I'm just asking questions," I said.

"They think you're a threat, you're on your own."

"What does that mean?"

"We're not bodyguards, you know. We can't protect you from yourself."

We'd reached the elevators. I stabbed the button. "Now that inspires confidence."

"Carry on," she said and headed along the corridor to parts unknown.

* * *

The sign on the door read Department of Planning and Community Development. I passed a counter that served as the reception desk, behind which a half-dozen people bustled between rows of flat drawers and stacks of file boxes. Everybody seemed to be moving these days. A smiling woman in a baby blue twinset waved me into Tamika's office and I prepared to be impressed.

I wasn't. The office felt cramped and cold as the snow forts we'd built as kids, the walls and carpet done in municipal beige. Books towered on chairs, rolls of paper leaned against the wall and plants crawled off the windowsill. Tamika's desk bristled with electronics, a monitor, notebook computer, tablet and phone competing for space. She'd squeezed the desk between a window that gave onto a courtyard and a wall-sized map of the city.

If the room looked chaotic, its resident didn't. Tamika Williams virtually glowed in a silver blouse with a large necklace made from agate. She rose to grasp my hand, her smile a broad and generous welcome.

"I like your glasses," I said as she offered me the only free seat in the house.

The glasses were stylish rectangles that coordinated with her jewelry. The spangle of freckles bridging her nose looked strategically placed to highlight the frames.

"I'm told they make me look professorial, which isn't a bad thing in this line of work." Hands splayed to the side, she tucked her chin and waggled her head, her long, straight hair waving with the motion. The effect reminded me of girls on the playground of my elementary school.

I declined her offer of coffee or water and handed the rental agreement across the desk. We sat. She reviewed the papers and punched something into what I assumed was her phone's calculator app. Then signing the sheets, she called for her admin, the bluebird I'd seen on arrival, and asked her to please photocopy the packet.

We talked about the apartment—she wanted to know if she could move some furniture before next month—until her admin returned with the rental agreement. Writing a check for the first month and last month's rent, Tamika returned the originals and, folding her hands on the desk, adjusted her collection of rings, bangles and bracelets and smiled.

It was my turn at bat. "Do you have a minute? I'd like to talk to you about Vertex."

"That's a relief. I thought you were here to lay claim to Mitch."

"Wow. That's direct."

"I understand you two had a relationship at one time."

I shifted in the seat, the synthetic weave scratching my slacks. "It ended a while ago."

"That's what Mitch said. Still." She let the word hang like a piñata. "You were very gracious to show us the apartments."

"All part of the job."

"Well," she said. "Now that I know *we're* not the issue, how can I help you?

"I might be able to help *you*."

She blinked but otherwise maintained her posture and poise.

"I understand you're in charge of reviewing all development plans for the city."

"And making recommendations to the commission, yes."

"What do you know about Ryan Donovan?"

"The young man who drowned?"

"I understand he talked with you about the geotechnical report on Vertex."

"I did meet with him, briefly. He wanted to share data he claimed wasn't in the final report."

"What data?"

"He said the tests revealed the possible intrusion of water into the carbonate rock."

She must have read my impatience because she raised a hand. "This can get a little technical, so bear with me. Florida's soil is a mixture of sand and clay that sits on top of the bedrock. You have organic material like grass on top; surface dirt, what most people call topsoil; subsoil, that's self-explanatory; and parent material, or bedrock, which in our case consists mainly of limestone."

"What was Ryan's concern?"

"Limestone is composed of calcite, among other compounds. It's a porous material that dissolves in water. The base on which these large multi-family complexes sit could erode when water penetrates the surface. That could form karst terrain, what most people call caves or sinkholes."

"So Ryan found evidence of sinkholes under what's going to be Vertex?"

"No," she said, "and I want to be clear about that. He presented data that he says contradicts the geotechnical report the construction company filed with the plans it submitted to the city."

"So no sinkholes."

"He seemed more concerned about potential water intrusion due to hurricanes and rising seas, although subsidence can be triggered by drilling or excavation. But we've seen no evidence of that, either in DeSoto Park or along the Route 41 corridor."

"The Tamiami Trail," I said. What does the contractor say?"

She forced a smile. "Was Ryan a friend of yours?"

"He was the nephew of a friend."

"I'm sorry if this sounds a bit insensitive, but Gulf Coast Drilling claims that Mr. Donovan doctored his figures in an attempt to damage the company. This was apparently in retaliation for a reprimand he'd received for violating health and safety rules." She waggled her head. "They stand by their data."

"I just had a conversation with Dean Caldwell, the construction manager of Vertex and InSpire. He gave the impression that, unless the city forces the issue, they're not going to check for anything."

"I'll review the original documents and, if I do find any anomalies, the city can ask the contractor to run some additional studies. But, as you can imagine, the contractor would dispute that, since the evidence your friend presented is hearsay. If I do find something, I can share that information with our codes enforcement officer. But, to be frank, our office is getting slammed. In the downtown alone, there are eighty-five projects in the development or construction phase—seventeen that we consider major projects, like the two you're involved with."

"And the city commission shows no signs of slowing down."

Raising her hands in a gesture of surrender, she leaned into the chair. "Above my pay grade."

"All I know," I said, "is that it doesn't pass the smell test."

She tapped the side of her nose. "We need more than a hunch to launch an investigation."

"What about Ryan? He reports what he thinks are suspicious numbers and the next week he drowns." I winced at the desperation in my voice.

"It's possible we're confusing correlation with causation."

"That doesn't make much difference to Ryan."

She sighed. "Without corroborating evidence, like a police report, we'd be exposing the city to years of litigation. I assume you've talked with your agency. What do they have to say?"

I reminded myself to breathe. "Nothing, although I doubt my boss would undermine her biggest project. Or her second biggest."

Tamika raised her brows.

"InSpire. That's what I tried to discuss with the construction manager. I understand subsidence can create small cracks in a foundation that even the trained eye can't see."

She rose to place a finger on the map. "What you're saying is that if there is subsidence here," she traced a line south from Vertex to DeSoto Park, "that it's likely to occur here."

"I checked the DEP maps and, when it comes to sinkholes, the Tamiami Trail is like the San Andreas Fault. How would you check those buildings for cracks?"

"The simplest way is through a visual inspection."

"The contractor says he hasn't found anything."

"There are nondestructive tests." She rattled them off with a roll of her hands. "Ultrasonic ping sensor, line or time-of-flight laser and camera, microwave imagining. If they discovered surface cracks, they might do core borings into the concrete itself. Although doing that on tower two, the residents of InSpire One would rightly want their building tested."

"Who could order those tests?"

"On the advice of our codes officer, our department would make a recommendation to the commission. But, again, we'd have to see the evidence." Her smile seemed genuinely apologetic.

"So now it gets political."

"Right or wrong, there could be repercussions, for the city and Thompson Partners."

"I saw Charles Palmer on the way in," I said. "Pitching it hard on CNBC."

"It's funny you should mention that. Someone from his office was here yesterday suggesting we include local stocks in our 401(k) because Spanish Point is," she curled her fingers, "'open for business.'"

"Which employee."

She waited a beat too long.

"Mitch."

She nodded. Now that the conversation had come full circle, it seemed like a good time to go.

"So where," I asked, "does that leave us?"

"I would need to see the data, something definitive, before we could take action. I have to be within the ninety-five percent confidence interval to take this to the commission."

She must have read the look of frustration on my face. "If you like, I could talk with the head of your agency about this."

My stomach lurched. "That shouldn't be necessary." Besides, I thought, her daughter screens her calls, and Melissa had issues.

The phone on Tamika's desk rang. She answered, checked the chunk of black glass on her wrist and said she'd be there in a minute. Escorting me to the door, she pumped my hand, thanked me for bringing the rental agreement and offered a business card.

She pointed to a number in the corner. "That's my personal cell. If you do come up with anything, please give me a call."

"Do you give this number to everyone?"

She waved a hand. "You'd be surprised at how many people have that number. I'll bet your boss has it on speed dial."

I didn't know why a real estate broker would need to call the planning department, unless said broker wanted to shape the very structure of the city. That answered my question. I held the card aloft as if it were a trophy and thanked Tamika for her time.

She ushered me along the corridor. "I'm sorry I couldn't be of more help."

"I guess I'm on my own."

Behind the wafer-thin lenses, her eyes appeared large and soft, maybe even sympathetic. "As the British like to say, mind the gap."

It could have been a warning not to mess with Thompson's people or just a cute expression. Given the rush of bodies in the office, I had no opportunity to find out. The admin in the blue twinset must have been working through the lunch hour. She hefted what looked like a platbook onto a table and blew hair from her eyes. Adopting my most sociable smile, I stopped across the counter and waited until she acknowledged me.

"If you don't mind my asking," I said, "who just called Ms. Williams?"

Looking me in the eye, she said she couldn't divulge that information.

"O for two," I said and showed myself out.

18.

"RAE, I'M SORRY, I'm really sorry."

"What'd you do now?" she asked, her voice like sandpaper.

Digging through the deodorant, sunscreen, napkins and wipes that littered the SUV's console, I found my hands-free device and jammed it in my ear.

"Rae, you still there?"

"In the flesh."

"I can't make the memorial service for Ryan. I have to take Pap to the neurologist. There's something going on with his medication."

"No problem. This is gonna sound terrible, but I don't want to be there, either. The church will be filled with a lot of people who mean well, and we'll have to stand in line for an hour and hug every one of them. It'll be exhausting, and Eddie's in no shape to meet and greet."

"How's he holding up?"

"He shut down. I can't blame him. I would, too, if I didn't have to handle the arrangements. You ever notice how this stuff always falls to the women?"

I had, but she had enough on her plate.

I asked if she needed anything. "Money, company, a hot dish?"

"Hot dish?" She laughed. "Since when do you cook?"

"It's been known to happen."

"I'll grab something at the restaurant."

"Speaking of work," I said, "how's the arm?"

"Getting there. The doctor says I've got a head like a rock. Probably broke the machine."

"There you go."

"Enough of the chitchat. What'd you find out this morning?"

Before the manic chase to Venice, I'd called to tell her about the pending visits to Dean and Tamika. She'd summarized her expectations with a snort, adding that she doubted I'd learn anything, self-interest always winning out over truth. Now I had to confess she'd been right and admit that I'd misjudged both people.

"That Caldwell guy," Rae said. "He sounds like a real sleazebag."

Inhaling deeply, I felt compelled to defend him. "He's just defending the company."

"Ryan lost his life. Did he think about that?"

"The subject didn't come up."

"What about that woman in city hall?"

"Tamika? I don't know if she can do anything," I said. "At least she was sympathetic."

"That'll help," she said and disconnected.

* * *

I drove west on a street that wound through oaks so heavy with moss it resembled tinsel on a Christmas tree. As I rounded a corner, the canopy suddenly opened to reveal the gray blue waters of the bay, crouched like a lion stalking prey.

Last month, when back-to-back hurricanes had hammered Spanish Point, I hadn't waited for the roads to clear to check on Pap. Commandeering one of the detective's SUVs, Cheryl had driven us around stacks of debris until the property hove into view. Despite its place on the water, the building remained unfazed. So had Pap. He'd lived through 2004's Hurricane Charley, the second costliest in U.S. history and one that had returned Punta Gorda to cattle pasture. Every storm had paled after that.

Harbor Acres looked placid today. With its green shutters, white porch and circular flower beds stuffed with geraniums, the complex looked more like a New England B&B than a resort for the aged. The lobby was spacious, the furniture new, the tile as polished as a mirror. I waved to the woman at the desk, took the stairwell to the third floor and knocked on Pap's door.

His jowls had sunk a bit and his ears looked a little bigger, but with his trimmed hair, apple cheeks and ready smile, he looked the spitting image of Tony Bennett in his eighties. Today he seemed alert and happy, the scent of Old Spice rising as I kissed his cheek. He'd donned his usual outfit to ward off the frigid temperatures of the doctor's office, a yellow golf sweater and stone-washed jeans that had faded to white on the thighs.

"Ready?" I asked.

In one hand he held an amber bottle of pills. "Should we take these?" he asked, his voice a low rumble, his speech as slow and deliberate as his movements.

I tapped the pocket that held my phone. "I've got the list of all your medications right here."

Neck immobilized by Parkinson's and arthritis, he looked through a pair of wild white eyebrows and tried to smile.

* * *

The temperature in the neurologist's office had dropped to something between freezing and absolute zero. Even the woman at the reception window wore a sweater. I checked in and seated Pap away from the TV. While they hadn't tuned the set to the usual news or police dramas, the compressed sound of the commercials could peel an eardrum.

I rummaged through a pile of *Time*, *Field & Stream* and *Highlights*. "Would you like a magazine?" I asked, knowing he had more trouble with boredom than reading.

Peering through amber aviators, his eyes wide and watery, he smiled. "No, thank you."

We sat for seventeen minutes and thirty-four seconds, not that I was counting, when a woman I assumed was a med-tech called Pap's name in a tone she'd reserved for the annunciation—far too cheerful for what went on in the office. Castigating myself for the surly attitude, I helped Pap to his feet. Hunched over himself, he made small, shuffling steps, his arms curving inward, fingers pinched at the tips—a motion the doctor called the Parkinson's gait. As we passed through the door, I smiled and thanked the tech. It wasn't her fault that Pap had contracted this disease. It wasn't Pap's fault, either. Not that any of this self-talk did anything other than drive me nuts.

The exam room consisted of a table the doctor never used and two chairs positioned opposite each other. Although the room wasn't as cold as reception, I tugged Pap's shirt and sweater closed, pulled another chair to his side and waited. Within minutes the neurologist arrived. She was from Goa, a small, bright-eyed woman with high cheekbones and dark hair pulled into a ponytail. She smiled, shook my hand and, clipboard balanced on a knee, spent the rest of the session speaking directly to Pap—one of the reasons we kept returning.

She asked him to name the day, date and their location as well as the name of the president of the United States. Slowly, he did. She asked him to count backward from one hundred by sevens. As he spoke, I silently followed, getting tangled as we approached the sixties. Pap did well and earned a smile and a notation by the doctor on her clipboard.

The hard part came next. She asked about his condition, which seemed to drop and plateau with each new procedure or medication. Pap tended to minimize his symptoms, as if he didn't want to inconvenience the doctor. This was one of the few times she turned to me, the independent observer and bearer of bad news.

I started with the small inconsistencies. Sometime Pap would reach for a word and settle on a familiar substitute, like Orlando for oregano. Other times a look of bewilderment would cross his face as he searched, as if rooting in the bottom of a drawer for a missing pair of socks. Then there were the more problematic lapses, the times when the one-two punch of Parkinson's and Alzheimer's corrupted both his vision and memory and he saw Grandma Alma at the foot of his bed, as if she'd just dropped in for a visit. Like smoke, his memory would drift, a tendril he'd grasp only to discover air.

The doctor nodded, confirming the observations with Pap, who took it stoically. She said that carbidopa/levodopa, the medication that greased his wheels, could, in larger doses, cause hallucinations, and she reduced his. She judged his mental acuity where she'd expect it and left the other medications unchanged.

Standing, she placed a hand on Pap's forearm. "You're doing well. We will see you in two months."

The billing clerk was courteous, the waiting room full, the parking lot ablaze with cars. I bundled Pap into the SUV and put the radio on low. As we pulled into traffic, Scotty McCreery sang about how he wanted five more minutes with the people he loved.

Wasn't that a bitch.

* * *

The woman at the desk of Harbor Acres seemed genuinely pleased to see us, addressing Pap by name and reminding him about a dance in the lobby after dinner on Sunday. "We'll have a live band, and you can even have a beer."

"Maybe I should move," I said and watched a smile stretch his face.

In his room, Pap settled into a creased leather recliner I'd brought from the house and asked if I could get him anything. He said no and waited for me to say what I'd come to say. From a pocket I removed a slim packet of love letters my father had written to my mother when they were young, letters Pap had given to me years ago but that, until recently, I hadn't read. Perched on the side of the bed, holding the letters in my lap, I asked Pap to tell me about my father.

I'd sat directly in front so he wouldn't strain to see, yet his rheumy eyes took in most of the room as if trying to locate the voice. Swallowing, he finally spoke, the words sounding like a loud whisper. "I wasn't sure you wanted to know."

I wasn't either.

"You know most of it."

"I do," I said. "All except why."

"There's not much to tell."

He was right. To paraphrase the stilted language of the police report, Ward McCoy, age thirty-two, and his wife Catherine, age thirty, had walked from their home to a party at a neighbor's house. They'd left their two children, Colton, age seven, and Candace, age five, at home, in the care of Ward's parents, Arthur and Alma Ward, something the couple had done on several occasions. The couple left the party on foot at 11:40 p.m. and arrived home shortly before midnight.

That's when the narrative frayed. Sometime after midnight, the county control center received a report of a house fire on the 800 block of our street. A witness said she saw a man matching my father's description running down the street. When firefighters broke into the house, they found the kitchen ablaze, my mother in a fetal position near the stove. She'd been struck in the head with a blunt object. Both she and my brother succumbed to smoke inhalation. Firefighters ran a ladder to the second floor and pulled me from my bedroom.

It was a clinical report, devoid of trauma, and answers.

All I could remember was darkness thick as a blanket and the fist of smoke in my throat. A fireman dressed like a scuba diver broke my bedroom window to carry me down a ladder that rocked and clanked. And then the warm smell of my grandmother as she cradled me on the ride to their home.

I blinked myself out of the reverie. My voice, when it came, sounded flat. "What happened when they got home? Did they argue? Did he threaten her?"

"Your grandmother and I thought everything was normal."

"He never said anything beforehand, anything to indicate. . . ." I couldn't finish the sentence.

"Your father was a very private person."

"That doesn't explain what he did to Mom and Colt."

He managed an apologetic crease of his mouth.

"It wasn't your fault," I said. "Or Grandma Alma's."

"It wasn't yours, either."

Pocketing the letters, I said I had a showing but that I'd stop by on Sunday to hear the band. Elbows jutting, he planted both hands on the arms of the chair and struggled to rise. When I'd gotten him upright, he stooped to pick with clawed fingers at something on the carpet.

"What is it, Pap?"

"The cleaning people. They're always leaving scraps of paper."

"Pap, there's nothing there."

He straightened as far as he could and slowly shook his head, as if he should know better.

It broke my heart.

19.

"YOU'RE HEALING WELL," Tony said as he drew me in for a kiss on the cheek.

"Thank you," I said, the flush above my collarbone spreading to my neck.

His lips felt soft and warm, the hand on my arm strong and slightly possessive. Despite my conflicted feelings about Mitch, I'd looked forward to this evening, a time that promised to leaven the sadness of the past three days. A kiss-and-makeup date, one I hoped would lead to something other than interruptions.

"Keep it up," he said, pointing to the thin white scar that divided his chin, "and you'll wind up looking like me."

"I should be so lucky."

That drew a smile.

"How's the leg?" he asked as we climbed into his ride, a white SUV the size of Texas, replete with cowcatcher and a nav unit an astronaut would envy.

I pushed the articulating arm of the computer toward the dash. "Serviceable."

"You get the bike back?"

"Tomorrow. If I can bum a ride."

He laughed. "I'm afraid you're on your own."

"What else is new?"

Humor sounded good on him. He looked good, too, fresh and showered in a crisp white polo and khakis, a glint of moisture sparking his dark hair.

We'd agreed to try the rooftop bar at one of the new hotels bordering the Intracoastal, a narrow skyscraper of concrete and glass that resembled a jeweled dagger. It offered a clear sightline to the bay—at least for now, until the condos of Vertex obliterated the view. We found a parking slot beneath the building, crossed a lobby with a wall of metal resembling a school of fish and took the elevator to the nineteenth floor. The doors opened onto a deck with a pool on one side and umbrella tables, couches and canopy gliders rimming the edge.

The place was crowded so we took padded stools at the bar, scanned the drinks menu—beachy concoctions like hard lemonade dominated—and asked about the drafts, forgoing the usual suspects like Stella and Blue Moon for a regional IPA called Jai Alai.

"You can't get more Florida than this," I said and raised a glass.

"You ever try the gator stew at Myakka?"

"It's a treat," I said, remembering a trip with Spanish Point Police Officer Skip Taggert that could have ended with me swimming with the animals.

"How did the showing go?"

I'd texted him earlier when I thought I'd be running late.

"Cash deal," I said. "We close within the month."

"How about the new listing?"

The rising level of noise forced me to lean close, bracing a hand on his arm for balance. "Are you ready for some irony?" I paused for effect. "Lois Danforth."

"Walter's friend." His voice, low as a bass drum, vibrated my ear.

"She's moving north to live with relatives and wants to sell the place as-is."

"Trouble?"

"Just the opposite. It's a Mediterranean revival, four beds, three-and-a-half baths , three-car garage, on a third of an acre of grass—although why Lois needed all of that space, she wouldn't say. The bathrooms and pool need some updating but, other than that, the place is in great shape. The comps came in at six and a quarter but Lois wants to sell as-is. At $575,000, it's the least expensive home in the community."

He nursed his beer. "What's an average house go for these days?"

"The ask is well above the median for the county—about two-ninety the last I looked—but it's half of new construction. And don't even think about finding a place on the keys for under a million or two."

"What's it like?" he said. "Working with a friend as a client?"

The surprises kept coming. Unlike a lot of men, Tony paid attention. He worked the conversation. Maybe God was in His heaven and all was right with the world, at least our little piece of it.

"Lois walked me around the neighborhood. Other than a run to the grocery store, I think it's the first time she's been out since her sister died."

The maître d, a stick of a woman clad in black Spandex, gestured toward the tables and asked if we had a preference.

Tony pointed to one of the hanging chaise lounges. "You want the hammock?"

I laughed. "With my luck, I'd topple over the edge."

We took an umbrella table near a clear plastic sheet that fenced the perimeter, Tony with a steady hand at the small of my back, "So you don't fall." The attention felt good. He assumed his usual position, back to a wall so he could keep an eye on the room, fluffed a napkin and laid it in his lap. The waiter, a tall man with hair as black as Tony's, arrived. His name was Rafael and he was from Ecuador. Tony gave him a nod and we listened to the specials, many of which involved fish we'd have to debone ourselves.

With a bow, the waiter left. We glanced at the menus but gave most of our time to the bay, with its boats floating like toys in a bathtub, the sun sliding behind the condos that lined the keys.

Rafael reappeared with bread and water. We ordered—filet for Tony, grouper for me—and when the waiter left, I leaned forward to ask Tony about the mad bombers.

"Any luck in tracking the fugitive?"

"Venice PD pulled that one."

"But it started here."

"We caught the robbery."

"I hear they have ties to New Generations."

Tony broke a piece of bread. "Phil Cunningham's charity."

"The bar chase was a hit."

He lifted a water glass halfway to his mouth. "What are we talking about? The bike accident?"

"That was no accident."

"You have proof?"

I sat back. "You know I don't."

He returned the glass to the table. "I thought we weren't going to talk shop."

"Only when I'm personally involved."

"When aren't you personally involved?" He rattled off a list of names, extending a finger with each one, starting with my grandfather and ending with a police officer who'd barely survived an internal investigation.

The food arrived, enough for dinner and two lunches. I asked for another draft. Tony stretched a palm over the top of his glass. We arranged plates and silver and tucked in, alternating salad with the main course.

"All right," I said, savoring the salty bite of blackened fish. "Change of subject. What about the death of Ryan Donovan?"

As Tony sliced his filet into thin strips, a shadow crossed his face. "It's not my case."

"You guys ruled it accidental."

"It was accidental. And, it's not my case."

Undeterred, I summarized my conversations with Dean and Tamika.

"It sounds," he said, "like a disgruntled employee getting even."

"It sounds like a cover-up."

I'd finished my second beer. Tony's glass was still half-full. He chewed, sipped water and dabbed his lips with the napkin.

"What about Casey and Melissa? Did the detective what's-his-name trace their movements?"

Tony sighed. "Melissa Cunningham followed him but turned back. She would have been home at the time of death. Gatehouse records confirm it."

"And Casey?"

"She says she spent the night with her husband."

"Phil?"

He folded his hands. "Disappointed?"

"In more ways than one."

"Your turn," he said. "Who's your source?"

"I can't say."

"If your boss finds out. . . ."

"I know."

"Risky," he said.

"What isn't?" I put a lot into the smile but I don't think he read it properly because he asked about Tamika Williams.

"Did she tell you that she'd look into the Donovan kid's report?

"No," I said. "Not really. Maybe. I don't know."

He scraped the inside of a foil-covered potato. "You're coming up snake eyes."

"I didn't think you were a gambling man."

"You have to be in this business."

"Which is as good a reason as any for dessert."

He raised a hand, and I could see a future judge calling for order in his court. "I thought you might like to walk the beach."

"Why, Tony." Maybe the smile had worked. I tried batting my eyelids but the lumpy brow hurt. "I never knew you were such a romantic."

"Don't get your hopes up." He patted his stomach. "I need to work off dinner."

The sad truth was, my hopes had risen, and if it hadn't been for the drowsy warmth created by the meal, I might have gotten upset. Tony signaled for the check. I let him pay. We rode the elevator to the parking deck and had just climbed into his SUV when the radio squawked with the voice of a female dispatcher.

"Ten-32, Spanish Point Marina, southwest 41."

A reported drowning near Route 41, close to the slip where Walter berthed his boat.

Clicking the truck's ignition, Tony palmed the mic. "Dispatch. Six eighty-six."

"Six eighty-six, what's your twenty?"

As he gave our location, I heard the door to a romantic evening slam shut.

"There's no other detective on duty?" I asked.

He pointed to the onboard computer I'd shoved toward the dash. "No one else this close."

"OK," I said and buckled the seatbelt. "Let's roll."

Jamming the shift lever into park, he hung the SUV over the lip of the garage. "You'd be safer here."

"Seriously?"

"I'm not supposed to carry civilians."

I pounded his thigh. "You will if you want to walk without bending over."

He hit the rack lights and peeled rubber down the Trail.

20.

INCHING THE SUV through the parking lot, Tony stopped at the embankment that buffered the boats from the highway and keyed the mic.

"Dispatch. Six eighty-six, 10-20 at the marina."

"Six eighty-six, 10-20," the female dispatcher acknowledged.

Despite the hour—it had to be going on ten—the Spanish Point Marina blazed with light and sound. The flashing racks of half-a-dozen patrol cars weren't the only excitement. Sailboats streamed in from extended sunset cruises. Yachts rocked in their slips. The tourist barges slid through the channel, their palm-lined upper decks lit like Christmas.

Even with the windows raised, the place sounded like Mardi Gras.

Opening the door, I stepped into a crowd as thick as tar—suits emerging from the restaurants, flowered shirts and golf hats from the tiki bar, tank tops and shorts streaming into the marina's park from hundreds of condos across the Trail. The curious clustered near the west end of the pier, held back by a cordon of officers, but the people aboard the yachts glanced at the traffic and lights and returned to their parties, leaning against metal rails with glasses held high as if to salute the warm October night.

Near the water, chaos reigned. Dinghies shuttled cargo to and from the bigger boats in the anchor field. Motorboats throttled, greasing the air with a mix of oil and gas. A Jet Ski darted between the barges, roiling the water, despite the signs that declared the marina a no wake zone. Maybe the rider couldn't read them in the dark.

I felt Tony's presence on my left.

"What ever happened to our retirement city?"

"Another myth." Tony sniffed. "Stay here."

Saying "excuse me," he pushed toward the bay. I followed.

No time for crime-scene tape, Patrol officers held the crowd with extended arms. Cresting the low hill, Tony stopped to speak to one of the officers, a tall blonde with a serious face and biceps to match. I'd seen her on TV, an up-and-comer who'd become the look of the department.

Tony asked if she was first on the scene and, when she said yes, asked about the victim. The officer gave me the cold eye but when Tony didn't explain my presence, focused on him. "Female, African-American, late twenties or early thirties, in full business dress." She pointed toward the shoreline between the edge of the docks and a peninsula stacked with condos. There were no lights, the basin an unbuildable plot that gathered debris and flooded with every rain.

A group of crime scene techs struggled past and began erecting tripods of portable lights, their bio suits glowing like ghosts. They were followed by the boxy red ambulance of Fire/Rescue and, finally, the bearded photographer who'd worked the Ryan Donovan scene.

Patrol hadn't tarped the body yet, but all I could see from here was a dark shape lying on the mudflat.

"Stay put," Tony said and headed down the slope.

The blond officer gave me the deadpan stare that dared me to defy her authority. But a trio of kids with dreadlocks and skateboards distracted her, and when a middle-aged couple demanded to know why they couldn't board their boat, I vaulted the steps to the dock for a closer look.

The pier consisted of concrete runways shaped like the letter T, with bars top and middle, the slips extending into the bay like fingers. Reaching the edge, I hung over the railing and looked down into a now-familiar face.

"Dear Jesus," I said.

Tamika Williams lay on her back, water sloshing against her left side, her hair fanning like seaweed. She was still dressed for the office, her jacket twisted, the silk blouse muddy but intact. Her skirt had ridden past her thigh to reveal a long scrape. She was missing her glasses, and one shoe. And her necklace.

Tony caught my eye and frowned but didn't order my ejection. I pointed to Tamika's skirt and made a motion with my finger to indicate he should pull it down. He nodded once and scanned the mob in the parking lot, telling the photographer to get some crowd shots when he was done. "And no strobe."

Circling the body in a wide arc, he signaled for the blonde officer to join him. They huddled. She pointed past the tethered vessels to the larger boats in the anchor field. He followed her gaze and nodded before joining me at the foot of the pier.

"Is it Tamika Williams?" I asked.

"No ID, but we think so."

"Is there anything I can do?"

"You spoke with her this afternoon. Did she say where she was going?"

"No. She got a call and said she had to run. Her admin might know."

We watched as the techs scoured the muddy bank as if searching for a missing contact lens.

"What do you know about her?" he asked.

"Very little."

"What about her personal life? Friends, boyfriends."

I felt a pang that reached deep into my chest. Reluctantly, I told him about the hunt for an apartment and her relationship with Mitch. The news would devastate him.

"What else was she working on?"

My dinner wasn't settling. "I couldn't say. Any idea what happened?"

Hands on hips, he stared across the bay. "Could have been a party, or a fight. Maybe whoever pushed her overboard, if she was pushed, didn't intend it. You met with her. You see anything?"

There was no point in withholding information that could lead to her killer. "Her necklace is missing."

"I'll tell the techs."

From the open-air restaurant, the music of a live band boomed across the water, competing with shouts and laughter, the splash of water and the growl of the outboards, sounds bouncing from the condos to gather in the basin like debris.

I waved toward the boats. "Who would leave her to drown? And what about these people? No one saw anything?"

"We'll knock on doors, but you've been inside these things." He nodded to the yachts closest to the anchor field, some large enough to ply the ocean. "They're buttoned up pretty tight."

I watched the partygoers in bathing suits and summer hats, all but those on the western edge of the pier ignoring the police activity. I pointed to the condos that lined the bay. "What about them?"

"At night, with all this traffic, you look out from the eighteenth floor and you can't be sure what you see, someone swimming, somebody drunk."

I see nothing, I hear nothing. The cop's lament.

The photographer had finished, the techs pulling a shroud over Tamika's body. She had died on an insignificant rim of dirt lapped by water slick with plastic and oil, iridescent in the artificial light, a light that would disappear with her. Walter would have checked this maudlin streak in me. Walter, the voice of contemplation and balance.

"It's not your fault," Tony said.

"How do you know that?"

"Because if you'd known there'd be trouble, you wouldn't have put her at risk."

The slip that held Walter's boat remained an empty hole. If he were here, what would he say about my meeting with Tamika and her death? What was I missing?

Two men in white shirts from Fire/Rescue lifted the body onto a gurney.

Police were diverting traffic from the parking lot, all except a white van with the logo of the Gulf Coast News Network. Two people slid out, the camerawoman who'd covered the Vertex groundbreaking and Leslie Ann Roberts. Their attention seemed obscene.

"Here they come," I said.

Tony turned, hand tented over his forehead, the crime-scene lights casting hard shadows across a worn face. "I'm gonna be tied up for a while. Can you find your way home?"

"Sure."

I resisted the urge to touch his arm. It wouldn't be appropriate, not here, maybe not anywhere. We hadn't had time to develop a relationship. I liked him. I admired his focus, his intensity, his sense of right and wrong. If we stayed together, I could adjust my expectations to enjoy method and order. I just didn't know if that was enough to satisfy this illogical craving for adventure.

Heading for the bay, he cocked his pinky and thumb like a set of horns and held them to his ear, mouthing "call me" before huddling with the techs. I retreated to the trees that lined the parking lot and punched the ride-sharing app on my phone, hoping that Hud was off duty. I didn't feel like sharing tonight.

21.

THE RIDE-SHARE DRIVER who took me to the garage the next morning did not feel compelled to recite his life history. At first I felt relieved, then disappointed, as if denied the full experience.

The garage was a tire franchise that did repair and body work on the side. It consisted of a cement-block building with six bays, a metal roof and a coffee machine that dispensed recycled motor oil. The business logo was a flying foot. An empty promise, if service so far was any indication.

I wasn't going to complain. Eddie Donovan had gone through enough this week. He owned the shop, the main reason I did business here, as well as the franchise on Cirque Nouveau and a half-dozen other eateries around town. That he still showed for work told me more about the man then a million reviews on Yelp.

My problem wasn't the service—the staff was disorganized but polite. It was me. Already late for a meeting at GHQ, I'd miss the update on Vertex preconstruction pricing. Even with a hundred agents in the room, Melissa would notice my absence and report me to her mother. In their world, tardiness was a mortal sin and missing an all-call worse than arriving late for a showing. Not for the first time I wondered how long I'd last in that corporate environment without strangling someone.

Eddie must have heard me check in because, emerging from his office, he rounded the counter and wrapped me in a bear hug. He went about two-eighty and carried most of it in front. When he stepped back, I took stock of the damage. His face was stubbled, his eyes as red as his hair and he smelled of old cigar. As usual, he'd dressed in mechanics gray.

"You look like hell," I said.

"Look who's talking."

He accepted my condolences, apologized for the wait and disappeared into the shop to see about the bike.

The waiting room consisted of plastic bucket chairs, an end table overflowing with year-old issues of *Car and Driver* and a wall-mounted television tuned to *Good Morning America*, where every segment revolved around product placement. On the counter, someone had placed a facsimile of a hand grenade with a card that read "Complaint Department: Pull for Service."

Out of respect for the owner, I decided not to complain. Sitting away from the TV, I produced a notepad and pen and reviewed the week's events. Tamika's admin had been as tightlipped as Walter's state police buddies. Even after identifying myself as a former LEO, they'd shunned me. No joy in either place.

I called Tony. He apologized for stranding me at a crime scene. "I figured you'd understand."

I did, all too well—another reason I had some doubts about a relationship. "What can you tell me about Tamika?"

"Just what we released to the media."

I'd read the newspaper account of the incident, then switched to the SPD website for the release. The police had little to offer. They were canvassing the marina and condos and interviewing Tamika's coworkers. SOP. Not that they would discuss an active investigation. Still, I was hoping for more, and asked if they'd found anything this morning at the marina.

"We can't search every boat."

"Maybe it's not a coincidence."

"The Donovan kid?"

"Two drownings in four days?"

"It's early. I'll call you."

"Better," I said and disconnected.

I was still preoccupied with Tamika, awash with guilt over the fact that I may have contributed to her death, when Eddie popped his head through the door to the service bays and told me my ride was ready.

The garage had pounded out the dents in the tailpipe and repainted the side. It looked as good as an antique could look. Given the time it took, the staff might have rebuilt the engine. But to their credit, they did make suitable noises of admiration when Eddie wheeled the Kawasaki into the lot.

I told him to leave it until I settled the tab. He waved me off. I thanked him with a hug, said how sorry I was about Ryan and that I'd continue looking into his death.

He pressed the keys into my palm. "Good hunting." His eyes shown with a fierce pain. "Isn't that what you're supposed to say?"

"I don't know what to say."

I left in a trail of blue smoke, cranking the bike on one of the cross streets that led to the bay, dipping through turns, weaving between cars before they slowed for the lights. It broke my heart to think of Tamika. I'd waited until this morning, until the police had time to notify Mitch, to offer my condolences. Like Eddie, he sounded numb.

And then there was Ryan. What were the odds of two accidental drownings involving the same project occurring in less than a week? I wondered, and not for the first time, if Phil Cunningham had anything to do with the deaths, and how much trouble I'd create if I accused him without evidence. Was I, as Cheryl had suggested, waging a vendetta, or was hizzoner getting special treatment?

And where during this mess was Walter? He was my rock, the person who stayed my hand during my manic phase and gave it strength when I fell into a black hole. Where had he gone, and why, and what was the smug Deputy Parrish trying to hide?

Approaching the downtown, I caught the flashing lights of the patrol car in the rearview and swore. Signaling, I pulled near the sidewalk, searched for the paperwork and, having located it, waited with both hands in plain sight.

The cop had angled the car into the passenger lane to block traffic. The door opened and Officer Charles Stover appeared. He approached the bike from an oblique angle and stopped slightly behind, forcing me to twist to see him. His face looked flat.

"Charles."

"CW. You know the drill."

I handed him my license, registration and insurance card. He retreated to the cruiser and, within a few minutes, returned with a sheet of thermal paper with my stats, a citation number and the details of the moving violation.

"You were fifteen miles over speed limit. I wrote it up as nine so the fine will only be $131 instead of 263. You have the option of contesting it, or paying the fine and having three points on your license. Or you can pay the fine and go to traffic school."

"Traffic school."

"It'll run you twenty-five bucks or so but it'll take the points off your license."

"Thank goodness for small mercies."

"At least I'm not making you walk the line."

"I'll give you that."

He returned my credentials but didn't move. "I hear you're looking into what happened to Tamika."

Sweat had broken out on his face.

"How'd you know that?"

"You wanna let us deal with it." He said *wiff* instead of *with*, the Philadelphia street kid coming out in his speech. Had circumstances been different, I would have followed Cheryl's lead and considered it endearing.

"Is that what you'd do, if you were me?" I asked.

"Not about me."

"No, it's not."

I stowed the paperwork and said I had to get to work.

He eyed the street as if daring it to start something. "You might want to go easy."

"I take it we're not talking about the bike."

With a nod, he walked to the cruiser, killed the lights and slid past.

I checked my phone and scrubbed several text messages, in order of increasing hysteria, from Melissa. While angry at the traffic stop, I was furious at myself for ignoring the law and giving my boss yet another excuse to bust my chops. Because compared to Casey Laine, the cops were a piece of cake.

22.

THE ALL-CALL MEETING had begun precisely at 9 a.m. I knew this because the minute I walked into the office, Casey passed before me like a wraith with spiky hair and barked, "Good of you to show."

"At least you're in time to meet Joe Lunch Bucket," Melissa said and trailed after her mother.

Ah yes, the hardhat tour of InSpire Two, yet another opportunity to mix with Dean Caldwell and the protesters across the street. I didn't know which was worse. The good news was that, while I hadn't had time to change out of my motorcycle gear, at least I was dressed for construction work.

Seated at my desk, I reflected briefly on my tenure at Laine & Company, or life in the fishbowl. I'd been assigned to headquarters with the task of selling condominiums. I knew the real reason I'd been moved from the 'burbs of Braden Ranch. Casey wanted to keep an eye on me. No more long lunches and freelance investigations. Butts in the chairs and phones at the ready. All the more reason to look busy.

Ranging through my contact list, preparing for the dreaded cold calls to scare up more listings, I watched the agent who sat opposite my station. She was one of our newest, a transplant from New York City who dressed exclusively in black and wore heels that could drive roofing nails. She was using the reflection of the computer monitor to refresh her makeup. Given the bruises forming on my face, I should have asked for pointers.

I didn't have time. Reception buzzed my phone to announce a visitor, "a Mr. Hudson from the ride-share company. Shall I send him back?"

"Why not?" I said.

It took him a while to navigate the slick porcelain floor but soon he clanked into view, the other agents staring without appearing to turn their heads. Miss New York gave him a smile reserved for clients she intended to poach. I returned the favor by asking if we could borrow her desk chair. There was only one, and she occupied it. Her smile froze. She suggested I could use the conference room. When I didn't move, she asked if she could get my guest anything from the kitchen.

"No, thanks," we said in unison.

Hud dropped into the chair and bumped his crutches against the desk. "Who's that?"

"That's Elaine from Manhattan."

"'Ooo wah, ooo wah cool, cool kitty. Talkin' about the girl from New York City.'"

"Right." I took in a lungful of air and caught the faint whiff of garlic.

Melissa rounded a corner, spotted us and doubled back.

"Hud, I appreciate your devotion to the cause, but you shouldn't just drop in here."

He pointed toward the lobby. "You see that beauty out front?"

Resigned to my fate, I leaned into the chair and prepared for the lecture I knew would follow. "A ten-foot barge is hard to miss."

"Barge? You're kidding me. You know what that is? That's the *Bluenose*. You know, the famous racing rig? Fastest fishing schooner in the North Atlantic. Dominated the sport in the nineteen twenties. The Canadians love it. They even put it on a stamp. Your boss Canadian?"

"Only when it closes a deal. Are you a fan of regattas?"

"Nah, can't stand water, all that rock and roll, makes me seasick. You think you could take a picture of me out front with the schooner?" He rattled his crutches. "Selfies are kinda hard with these."

I took a breath. "How did you make out with the carrying charge?"

"Apparently I'm covered under the Good Samaritan rule."

"I'm not sure there is one."

"Don't worry. I've got people looking out for me."

I doubted that. The incident forced me to rethink our relationship, if we had one. While I wanted to ask if he knew anything more about Ryan or Tamika, I didn't want to encourage or endanger him. He could get hurt just by asking questions. And visiting here without a checkbook.

Someone moved near the lobby, Melissa floating in the background like a shadow while agents gathered for the walk to InSpire.

"You didn't come here for a history lesson," I said. "Is there something I can do for you?"

"It's what I can do for you." He paused for effect, treating me to a smile as wide as the space between his teeth.

"You have something on Ryan Donovan."

"Better."

"You know who killed Tamika Williams."

"Better yet."

As I leaned back, the chair groaned. I knew how it felt.

"You wanted to know about the boat guy, Walter somebody?"

I waited. Unlike football, there was no hurry-up signal for a conversation.

"You ready for this?"

"Gary, before I turn old and gray. . . ."

"Hud. Everybody calls me Hud."

"About that. . . ."

"His boat'll be here this weekend."

My stomach tried to climb my throat. "Who's boat?"

"That friend of yours, Walter somebody."

"How do you know that?"

"Word on the street."

I leaned forward quickly enough to startle him. "Whose word?"

"Some fare I picked up near St. Pete."

"What did he look like?"

The description could have fit Parrish or a dozen others.

"He told you Walter was arriving this week?"

"He was on his phone. You know fares. They pretend no one's listening and get miffed if you do, so you have to act like you're not."

I rose and felt my pockets for the keys to the bike.

"Where're you going?"

I intended to pay another visit to Deputy Parrish and wring the information from him if necessary. But walking by my desk Melissa said "fifteen minutes to show time" with a forced cheer that made me rethink my impulse to leave.

Levering himself from the chair, Hud collected his crutches and turned to leave. "I think someone's trying to get your attention."

I was considering whether I could work from home when Melissa handed me a paper that turned out to be the morning's agenda.

She tracked Hud's jerky movements through the lobby. "Who's your fan?"

Her cheeks looked puffy and her stomach bulged. This from a woman who weighed herself before applying deodorant. Usually she looked as if she were strutting a runway. Not today, and I doubted it was the garden-variety trouble with men.

"He's a ride, not a fan."

Melissa pinched her nose, as if she'd smelled something obnoxious. "I don't care but Mom's annoyed. She think he's déclassé. Unless he wants to buy a condo. Then it's champagne and flowers and a night at the Ritz on us."

"Maybe I'll get him an apartment."

"For a five hundred dollar finder's fee? Who can live on that?"

"Speaking of money," I said. "Why is your father on CNBC promoting Thompson Partners? Charles Palmer, I can understand. He's got brokers in his office. But your dad?"

"He promotes the region, you know, economic development and all that crap."

"Does he have a lot of shares in Thompson's company?"

"Everybody does. I don't know diddly about stocks and even I own it."

"Saving for the future?"

"Saving for Mom. She makes us."

"Does she own a lot?"

"A shitload." Melissa fanned her arms to encompass the office. "How do you think she pays for this, and the villa in Italy, and the agencies she's snapping up in Naples and Palm Beach?" She pressed a hand to a mouth drawn broadly with lipstick. "I'm not supposed to tell you that. You won't tell her I told."

Her mood swings were becoming historic.

"No," I said, "but something's bothering you."

She folded her arms and took a step back. "Who said anything's bothering me?"

"I saw how you looked at the groundbreaking. You were upset. Does it have anything to do with your mother and Tommy Thompson?"

"Thanks to Tommy, we'll have money coming out our butts."

"I saw him slide an arm around your mom. Your dad didn't look very pleased."

"He's the one who walked out. Why should he care?"

"Your mother told me she was going to evict him."

"Whatever."

"If it's not about your father, is it about Ryan Donovan?"

She rubbed her hands as if to warm them.

"I heard he visited your home that night."

"Who said that? Mr. Gimpy?"

"Melissa, the gatehouse keeps track of these things. If I know about it. . . ." I let the statement ring the air like a bell.

She folded her lower lip under her teeth, tracing a burgundy line on the enamel. "You have to promise not to tell Mom. Cross your heart and promise."

"When did you see him?"

"The night he died. I mean, I wasn't with him when he drowned. I was still at the house."

"Your house?"

"I know, I am such a slut, but don't tell Mom."

I lowered my voice. "It's a question, Melissa, not a judgment. Did something happened between you two?"

Breath narrowed her nostrils to slits, a trait I'd noticed in her mother, and for a moment I thought she'd shut down. The she broke, her face collapsing with her voice. "We fought. It was stupid shit but they probably heard us in downtown Miami. Sometimes, when I get going, I can't stop, I just run off at the mouth until I say something completely stupid and then it's too late to ever take it back." She sniffed and dabbed an eye. "Not that that ever happens to you."

I thought of my confrontation with Lois over her desire to domesticate my seafaring friend and made a mental note to treat Melissa as a fellow sinner. "What did you two fight about?"

"He wanted to surf the jetty and I told him he might be a monster for that but I wasn't getting up at the butt-crack of dawn and hanging my ass over a board when there's a tropical storm fifty miles offshore dumping more rain than Irma and Harvey combined."

I doubted the accuracy of the assessment but appreciated her honesty. "What happened then?"

"He said we never get waves that big around here and I told him it was too freaking dangerous. He laughed and told me that I never took chances anymore, that my mother did everything for me, buying my car and my clothes and everything. He said I was becoming her Mini-Me. Besides, what did it matter what he did, nobody believed anything he said anymore, not even his own father, and now I didn't believe in him, either, so he might as well have some fun, even if that meant he'd have to hang out by himself."

"Did you go with him?" I asked.

She glanced over her shoulder, as if her mother would swoop down like the Wicked Witch of the West. "Hell, no. There was a shit-storm and it was still dark."

"That's not what you told the police?"

"What did I tell the police?"

"That you followed Ryan but couldn't find him."

Her face seemed to collapse. "He wouldn't be dead if I had."

"It's not your fault."

She looked behind again. "Everything's my fault these days."

"What about your mom? She wasn't home?"

Melissa wrung her hands. "She was out, God knows where. Do we really have to talk about this?"

I took in some air. "Did anyone else know where Ryan was going?"

She wrinkled her upper lip. "You mean, was he seeing someone else? How should I know? You think guys tell you that kind of stuff?"

"Did he say why he got let go from his job? What he knew? Why no one believed him?"

"He wouldn't talk about it. All he said was somebody in city hall had their head up their ass, and grabbed his board and took off."

"Did you mother know you were seeing each other?"

I seemed to have dropped back into cop mode and, from the look on Melissa's face, it showed, because she retreated another step.

"She's got other things on her mind."

I wanted to put this as carefully as possible. "What about your Dad?"

She must have run out of patience because when she glanced at the lobby her tone changed. "We're gonna be late."

I raised a hand. "One more question. Does Ryan's death have anything to do with Tamika Williams?"

A tremor shook her hands and she turned for her mother's office.

Now I've done it, I thought and, gathering my phone, headed for reception to join the crowd. There were at least a dozen of them, fellow agents staring at a widescreen mounted on the wall.

"What's up?" I asked Elaine from New York.

She balled her fists and tucked them under her arms. "It's more like what's down."

The agency's IT people had programmed the television to scroll images of featured homes. The feed consisted of luxury properties on the bay or the barrier islands. Someone had switched the channel to CNBC. At a desk that resembled a spaceship sat three of the program's anchors, a tanned man in a dark suit, a freckled one in a blue Oxford with the sleeves rolled and a pale woman in red. They were discussing whether investors had time to short the stock of Thompson Partners Inc.

"TPI has had a historic run," the woman said, "up more than three hundred percent in two years. Can we have the chart?"

"Until today," the blue shirt said. "Then kaboom! This one's headed for the basement."

Cue the graphic of TPI's price. The line resembled a cliff.

The camera cut to the anchor desk and the most sober-looking of the three. "Depending on whether Q4 earnings beat estimates, the stock could bounce."

"Dead-cat bounce," blue shirt said. "How can they be that far off? After last quarter's call, the CEO told anybody who'd listen they were booking record top and bottom line numbers. The Street's looking for EPS of a buck-forty a share and today they deliver half? What kind of guidance is that? And talk about a settlement package, a golden parachute? The CEO's lucky to get a bus ticket out of town."

The CEO was Tommy Thompson, who was about to discover that the market was as brutal as it was quick. I felt a momentary pang for him before remembering the slug of stock most of us had squirreled away in our retirement accounts.

The man in the suit touched his ear before squaring his jaw with the camera. "CNBC has just learned that trading in TPI has been halted."

I didn't know a lot about the market, that was Mitch's thing, but I knew the 401(k) was the least of our worries. If investor confidence tanked and the shares took a sustained hit, we agents might find ourselves selling fries.

At the sound of footsteps, I turned to see Casey. She drew back her shoulders and tipped her head to address the crowd.

"This is not our concern. Let's keep our mind on business. Remember the rules: if anyone from the media wants a word, you refer them to Melissa."

"Yes, ma'am," I said as we assembled for the march to the sea.

23.

"I NOTICED YOU were talking to Melissa," Casey said. She'd dropped to the back of the line where her comment wouldn't carry to the rest of the agents. "She seemed distressed. What did you say, if I might ask?"

"She did seem distressed. I was trying to find out why."

"And did she confide in you?"

"No, she didn't."

Conversation ceased as we breached the line of protesters who'd crowded the intersection. They parted for us, chanting "save our bay" and pumping the air with signs. As the lines folded into themselves, I spotted a familiar figure at the center — a red-face with flying hair. She'd painted her cast in the colors of the American flag and used it, along with her rusty voice, to rally the troops.

Rae Donovan returned my wave without breaking stride.

Casey gave the pickets a sour look. "Do you know that person?"

"I bump into her on occasion."

Casey gave the pickets her back. "What do they think they're doing here, besides making a nuisance of themselves?"

"I think they want to stop construction in the flood zone."

"I wish them luck with that."

We crossed the Trail into DeSoto Park, walking beneath the shade of ancient banyans to InSpire One. The police tape had vanished from the restaurant. In its place, a pair of fitters hefted a hurricane window over the sill, their grunts carrying on the breeze.

To the right, the crenelated floors of the second tower rose like a castle. So did the noise, the bang and clatter of progress. Cranes hefted beams, buckets dumped their slurry, rebar sprouted like petrified trees. The blocks that would house the elevators rose first, followed by five concrete decks, fringed in wooden forms. Bowlegged workers in orange hardhats straddled the beams as if navigating a ship.

A chainlink fence hung with green tarp kept onlookers at a distance. Dean Caldwell, clean, athletic, a fringe of gray peeking from his white hardhat, greeted us at the gate. He apologized for not allowing us into the building. "Safety rules," he said and nodded to a big man with a silver clipboard and shiny face who hovered in the background.

Keeping my voice low, I asked Casey if she recognized him.

"He works for the city's codes enforcement office."

"Routine inspection?"

"No inspection is routine."

Caldwell also apologized for not leading the tour and introduced his assistant, a redhead with straight hair that hung from the white hardhat like a flag.

Assuming her place in front of the line, Casey led us by a table ladened with plastic glasses of champagne. Even though I'd walked, I would take a pass. It seemed wrong to celebrate so soon after Tamika's death.

"Ladies, this is for after the tour," Casey said and led her merry band of swabbies into the shadow of the building, where the redhead rattled off statistics with remarkable speed and enthusiasm.

I noted that Caldwell hadn't looked in my direction. Nor had Melissa, who hung by her mother's side as if they were epoxied at the hip. I followed, which gave me a broad view of everything, including the street. Which is how I noticed the GNN news van as it spilled its contents onto the newly poured sidewalk—Leslie Ann Roberts and her crew.

"So we meet again," Roberts said, repeating an opening line she most likely used on everyone.

"Are you here to cover the protests or the tour?" I asked.

"We'll stretch a point and cover both."

Watching the tour disappear around the corner, I felt a growing sense of alarm.

She canted her head. Her lipstick matched her skirt, blouse and frosted nails. Her hair glowed like spun gold. "Do you mind if I ask you a question?"

I waited.

"Off the record?"

In my experience in dealing with journalists, there was no such thing as off the record.

"We should join the others," I said and began to walk.

Roberts trotted to match the pace. "Word has it you led the police to the Venice bombers."

Like a dark hand, a chill brushed my back. I presented a grim smile. "Whose word is that?"

"Is that a yes?"

"You'll have to take that up with the police."

"Who'd waste no time stonewalling the media to protect a friend?"

I'd never considered myself a friend of the department, just a few of the officers, but she might have a point, not that I would admit it.

"If this is an awkward time, why don't we meet for a drink?"

"You have a job to do but, off the record? It's career over if we talk."

Melissa peeked around the edge of the security fence.

"What about a trade?" Her breathing sounded labored.

Good, I thought and lengthened my stride.

"I hear you're still looking for your friend, Walter Bishop."

I stopped, forcing the camerawoman to swing wide to avoid a collision.

Roberts fixed me with glittering eyes. "I can help."

Adopting the stiff posture and language I'd practiced on the force, I told her the issue was in the hands of the police.

"We have contacts they don't."

As much as I wanted to trust her, I couldn't. Stalling, I looked toward the bay to see Melissa replaced by the pale figure of Casey Laine as she wobbled toward us on a pair of black heels.

I folded my arms. "Make it quick."

"I might need information on real estate and construction from time to time. Someone on the inside could help a great deal."

"There are a thousand agents with more experience."

"You're a former member of law enforcement. You have an in with the department. And whether you like it or not, you always seem to land in the middle of things."

Casey was closing fast.

"I'm not sure that's a ringing endorsement. Why are you really here?"

"Actually," Roberts said, "I'm here to see your boss."

She exchanged handshakes and smiles with Casey, who asked how she could help.

Roberts wanted an on-camera interview focused on the rapid growth of the downtown while touching on the opposition across the street. That issue settled, she reviewed the questions she would ask while the camerawoman clipped a mic to Casey's lapel and positioned her for the most flattering light. I'd been expecting an ambush, so this seemed downright civilized.

Casey fluffed the stalks of black hair over her forehead, tugged her jacket and looked into the camera. Roberts asked about the projects coming out of the ground and the ones in the planning stage, which included Vertex. When they'd settled into an amiable conversation, she asked about rumors of subsidence in the area.

Casey looked as if she'd been slapped. "You would have to speak to Tommy Thompson."

As a follow-up, Roberts asked if anyone had reported cracks in the foundation of InSpire and, if so, did Laine & Company know about the reports."

Casey's Adam's apple traced a fine line along her throat. "Again, you would have to speak with Mr. Thompson. But from our vantage, the city has thoroughly vetted both projects. These towers are built to Miami-Dade standards. They are designed to withstand a Category 4 storm. They are the safest buildings in the county."

Roberts inhaled for the next question but Casey, removing the lapel mic, said she was sorry but she'd said all she was prepared to say.

To her credit, she didn't tell Roberts to leave or offer to call the police.

I took a deep breath. Who had tipped the reporter to the story about subsidence? As I watched the pickets crowd the sidewalk, one name floated to the top of the list: Gary Hudson. I'd been indiscreet during one of our rides. In a misguided attempt to help, he'd taken matters into his own hands. Walking to the edge of the fence, I called Hud's cell. There was no answer. Part of me wanted to protect him. Another part wanted to wring his neck. Not wanting to leave a message, I disconnected. I got as far as the corner of the building when my phone buzzed.

"You rang?" he said over the noise of traffic and chants.

"Where are you?"

"Right across the street."

He stood on the corner, a tiny figure in a thick crowd, a bottle of water raised above his head in salute.

I wasted no time. "Did you tell Leslie Roberts about that report?"

"Is she as pretty up close as she is on camera?"

"Hud, you could get in serious trouble if people find out you leaked that information."

"Relax, the call was anonymous."

"No calls are anonymous."

"Hey, if there's nothing there, you guys have nothing to worry about."

"You're jeopardizing people's livelihood, people's careers."

"Somebody needs to check it out," he said.

"We have no evidence. All we have is the word of a young man who drowned."

"What about the stock?" he asked.

"What about the stock?"

"It's a classic pump-and-dump scheme. Some schmuck talks up the stock and, when everybody piles in, they sell before the news hits. Hey, the TV people are here and I need my fifteen minutes of fame. Gotta go."

He broke the connection. This was spiraling out of control. I needed answers. And I knew who had them. I just hoped he was still speaking to me.

24.

I BURST INTO Mitch Palmer's office to confront him about the stock trade only to find the floor deserted. While the parking lot and lobby of the blue tower brimmed with life, reception and the offices behind it appeared empty.

"Hello?" I yelled and wandered into the interior, my footfalls cushioned by thick carpet, the flicker of television screens following me like the eyes of the blind. Beyond the floor-to-ceiling walls of glass, sunlight danced on the bay. Sails dotted the water. Boats cut its surface. As usual, half of the world was ignoring what the other half was doing, much to its peril.

To my left sat the office of Charles Palmer, its space enclosed in heavy wood. A door opened and Mitch peeked through the opening. "It's you."

"Don't get all excited." I surveyed the empty desks. "Where is everyone?"

"Beating the bushes. Dad dispatched everyone to reassure the clients that the world isn't coming to an end."

"It's that bad?"

He pointed to the back wall where his father had mounted two large-screen TVs, one tuned to CNBC, the other to GNN. Judging from the closed-caption ticker, the GNN anchor was previewing an exclusive by Leslie Ann Roberts on whether possible defects at InSpire would halt construction of the project. Tonight at six on your Gulf Coast News Network.

"Chicken little," he said. "The market is falling."

"Great," I said, sensing the broadcaster's hysteria even without the sound. "Casey will love this."

"She's not the only one."

Mitch appeared worn around the edges, his face pinched, his hairline receding too quickly. The tie looked straight and the white shirt crisp but he never wore glasses unless his eyes were too tired for contacts, and he looked tired.

"I'm sorry to drop by unannounced," I said. "I wanted to offer my condolences in person. I know we just met but I really liked her."

"Thanks. I appreciate it."

Pointing to the television screens I asked, "Do you know what's going on?"

"You want something to drink? Soda? Water? We've got diet something-or-other in here."

He led the way to a space fitted with file cabinets, a photocopy machine and a kitchen complete with refrigerator, microwave, dishwasher and sink. Head disappearing into the 'fridge, he recited in a muffled voice, "We've got Diet Coke, Diet Pepsi, Red Bull, Mountain Dew, Monster and AMP. Pick your poison."

"So that's how you guys stay awake."

"The young guns like it."

I asked for water. He retrieved two bottles. They started to sweat, the cold plastic a relief against my skin. I thanked him. He led us to his glassed-in cubicle in the corner and offered me a seat with a pano view of the bay.

I told him I'd heard a rumor.

"That's a good start."

"About the stock of Thompson Partners," I said.

He made a clicking sound with his tongue. "With you so far."

The glass surface of the desk glowed—glass being de rigeur for the business class on the Gulf Coast. The desk contained a legal-sized piece of paper, a mechanical pencil with a black barrel and a tablet computer. Mitch leaned into a chair that could have cost more than I earned in a month and, like a chess player, waited for the next move.

"Last week," I said, "your father and the mayor were all over the airwaves promoting the downtown, and Thompson's stock."

"That's our job—attract investors to the Gulf Coast."

"Here's where it gets tricky," I said. "There's a report of possible ground subsidence beneath Vertex. Somebody alters the original report and someone else leaks that fact and, the next thing we know, the stock crashes."

"And wipes a couple million in value from our portfolios. Tell me about it."

"What if the person who altered the report found a way to make money on the trade?"

He leaned forward, his pale blue eyes ticking across my face. "You're saying someone traded on insider information and shorted the stock?"

"If that's what you call it."

"And you think this has something to do with us."

The room temperature dipped a few degrees.

"Last week, your father and the mayor went on national TV to promote Thompson Partners."

"We're boosters. That's what we do—promote regional business. Trickle-down two-point-o: a rising tide lifts all boats."

"An apt metaphor," I said. "You manage the mayor's portfolio."

"The firm does. Lots of them. We've got close to a billion under management. Where are we going with this?"

"Is there a chance the mayor's trying to cripple Vertex?"

He'd taken a slug of water and snorted so loudly he nearly spit on the shiny desk. "The guy's an investor. Why would he trash his own project?"

"I was hoping you could tell me."

"Did you read your own press release?"

He slid the tablet in front of me.

"It's not my release," I said. "Besides, I've been a little busy picking glass out of my face."

"I didn't say anything."

"I know you didn't, and you are a gentleman for not doing so."

The glowing screen showed the release that Melissa had distributed at groundbreaking. I flipped the tablet face-down and caught Mitch's eye.

"It says, and I'm virtually quoting here, that Vertex Spanish Point is a joint venture among Thompson Partners Inc., Founders Venture Capital LLC, Laine & Company and the City of Spanish Point. It is worth nearly half-a-billion dollars at buildout and will include a new arts, convention and visitors' center as well as retail, restaurants, hotels, condominiums and an expanded dock for boaters. Yada, yada, yada."

He appeared stunned or impressed, I couldn't tell, so I carried on.

"Skip to the end of this historic document, where we identify all of the players: Tommy Thompson as CEO of Thompson Partners, a public company trading on the New York Stock Exchange, ticker symbol TPI. Philip Cunningham, partner at Founders Venture Capital, and Laine & Company, one of the largest real estate brokerages in Florida, with nearly 1,000 agents and $3 billion in annual revenue. The family owned firm is led by its founder, Casey Laine. There is no mention of its cofounder, Mayor Cunningham. Apparently he's losing his stake in the divorce."

The plastic cover squeaked as I pushed the tablet across the glass surface.

Mitch sat back and tented his fingers. "I'm impressed."

At least he wasn't stunned. "But not enough to return my calls."

"OK, so I was a bit of a cream puff."

"Your dad put you up to it. It's that yacht thing, isn't it?"

He opened his palms to take in the room. "Hey, I'm on a short leash here."

I knew from the brief time we'd dated that Mitch didn't like making money for people who didn't use it to help others. If he could, he'd return to college and hang out with his fraternity buddies, build homes for Habitat for Humanity or take a job teaching kids closer to his age.

"I'm sorry," I said. 'Sometimes I get carried away."

His eyebrows rose but, God bless, he didn't agree, at least out loud.

I took a breath. "Why don't we start over. You were making a point about the press release."

"Let's play devil's advocate. Why, if the mayor's VC fund is bankrolling the project, would he trash the very company that's building it?"

"Because he tried to bury the ground-subsidence report and, when that failed, he had to get ahead of the news."

"Even if he did short TPI," Mitch said, "it's a legal trade."

"Unless he traded on insider information."

As if tasting something sour, he pursed his lips. "You'd have to work for the SEC. Dad isn't going to open the books to you or anyone else."

I leaned in. "What if Tamika was killed over that report?"

Palming the mechanical pencil, he tapped the desk, the eraser making a plopping sound on the sheet of paper. "It still makes no sense."

"Unless you've had a falling out with your partners."

"The divorce?" he asked.

"The affair."

"Now you're back to Susan Thompson."

"I'm talking about Tommy Thompson and *my* boss."

His eyebrows danced a jig. "That's a stretch."

"It's a theory."

He twisted the pencil. "It's libel."

"Slander," I said. "Libel is written defamation."

He raised three fingers and waggled them. "You're fishing."

"Can you just confirm the trade?"

"You know I can't."

I felt the blood rise in my face. "Who would know if you did?"

"As if that's the point."

"The point is that two people may have died because of this."

"You're looking for trouble."

"I'm looking for justice."

We stared at each other. I broke first.

"Can you at least tell me how something like this works?"

Mitch must have felt on safer ground because he stopped torturing the pencil. "OK. Let's say Investor X has a large position in a stock whose price has gotten ahead of itself. Overvalued, overbought, the price doesn't reflect the fundamentals. He can liquidate the position but, if the stock keeps going up, he misses out on the gains."

"So he buys some insurance."

"Close. He sells near the top of the market and takes a profit. But to stay in the game, he borrows shares from a lender, pays a small fee and sells those shares at the market price. Say he borrows a hundred shares of TPI and sells them for a buck a share."

"A dollar?"

"A hundred. Shares crater, he buys them back for a song, returns the shares to the lender, minus the fee, and pockets the difference."

"And if the stock price goes up?"

"It's a risky trade."

"Unless you know it's going to drop."

He spread his hands. The mechanical pencil came apart in two pieces.

"Do you know if the mayor has a boat?"

"A boat? Yeah. He's got a couple tied up at the house on the keys."

"How about the marina?"

"Look. I'll admit the mayor may have cut a few corners on his trades but the guy is a public figure. He's running for the statehouse. You don't get elected by murdering people."

"And you know this how? Because he and your father are golfing buddies?"

Slowly, Mitch shook his head. "You don't know this guy. Next to the governor, he's the top fundraiser in the state. Every developer, builder and broker has contributed to his campaign. He's got money and connections, and he's not afraid to use them."

I struggled to control my voice. "Two people may have died because of this deal. Someone has to stand up."

"Look, I want to know what happened to Tamika as much as you, but you've gotta get over this thing with Cunningham."

"You're trying to derail me."

"I'm trying to protect you."

"I don't need protection," I said and rose for the exit. "I need answers."

Passing the deserted reception desk, I thought about Hud's impulsiveness in calling the media and the restraining order the mayor had obtained the last time I'd questioned his motives. How much was I willing to sacrifice to bring the man to justice? If Walter were here, he'd tell me to steer clear. If I couldn't, he'd want me to work for the greater good. But in this case, what was the greater good?

I had three new listings to process and a showing of Lois's house. I promised myself I would put Walter's advice to the test. Just not today.

25.

"I'M ON MY way to the harbormaster's office," I told Cheryl by way of a cranky phone connection. "What can you tell me about the investigation?"

"Who put you in charge?"

I'd walked the two blocks from my office and paused at the intersection to wipe the sweat from my eyes. Not even noon and already the temperature had hit ninety. "Seriously. Walter's missing. Hud's gone rogue. Melissa's scared. The mayor's hiding something. And Tony won't tell me anything. Help me, Obi Wan, you're my only hope."

"You need to get a job."

"I have a job."

"You could've fooled me."

As I crossed the traffic circle fronting the marina, an SUV the size of an urban assault vehicle wheeled through the inside lane and nearly clipped me.

"Hey!" I shouted.

"Hey, yourself!" she yelled.

The SUV was a late-model Jeep with a Florida plate with the line "endless summer" and the silhouette of a guy with a surfboard. Clearing the intersection, I read the tag to Cheryl and asked if she'd punch it up on the squad car's computer. She wanted to know what had happened. I told her.

"The front bumper's smashed, on the driver's side, like the driver hit something."

"Where are you?" she asked.

I gave her the coordinates and looked for utility poles and lights. "There aren't any cameras here."

"Not at your end."

My end was near where Tamika's body had washed ashore. Unwilling to risk another encounter with traffic, I made for the sidewalk. "Where are they, the cameras?"

"Near the restaurant, so they can tell if the valets make off with a Beemer."

"No footage of the basin, then, or the docks?"

"Why make it easy for us?"

"It's city property. Why can't they install cameras?"

"The people who own those yachts? They like their privacy."

"So do I."

"They have money. You don't."

From here I could watch boats crowding the dock, their masts like a dancehall of chairs turned upside down. I heard Cheryl report the incident to Dispatch, the radio chatter filling my ear. I waited for the noise to subside. "Anything on the tag?"

"The vehicle was reported stolen this morning."

"And here I thought it was a tourist who didn't know how to navigate the roundabout."

"Careful," Cheryl said. "They're our bread and butter."

I'd reached the end of the L-shaped building that housed the pier's offices and restaurant and took refuge in its shade. "Getting back to Tamika. What'd the door-to-door turn up?"

"We went over that marina with a fine-toothed comb. Interviewed the boaters, pulled the fuel records, talked to a couple of condo owners, you know, the ones who walk their dogs at all hours so they can sort through their neighbor's trash."

"What'd they say?"

"Somebody saw a guy in a ball cap ditch a boat and run into the parking lot. They called the harbormaster and told him to tie off before it scratched their yachts."

"You find anything on the boat?"

"The techs are working on it. We ought to know by Christmas."

"Who owns the boat?"

"The harbormaster. At least that's what the paperwork says."

"You interview him yet?" I asked.

"Tony did. I hear his English needs work."

"Tony or the harbormaster?"

"It's too early for cute."

"What'd the harbormaster say?"

"He claims somebody borrowed the boat and didn't tie up when they brought it back. That's what he's worried about, dropping anchor."

"Who took it?" I asked.

"He doesn't know."

"You think he's telling the truth?"

"He's from Poland, over here on a visa. He's scared we're gonna yank it. You know him?"

"He's a friend of Walter's. I called after Walter took off. I think he'll talk to me."

"Just don't ask him out. We all know how your dates go." And with that she disconnected.

Visiting the harbormaster's quarters felt like revisiting the scene of a crime. In a way, it was. The place featured in a brawl I'd had with Cheryl's former husband, Sal. Even though that was in the security office next door, it still felt odd to walk into the place and have the same musty rush of conditioned air hit my face. Nothing else had changed. A 3-D relief of coastal shores carved in wood hung on one wall, a map of Europe with the borders of Poland outlined in red on the other. With glass windows and doors front and back, the place offered as much privacy as my new digs. I said hello to an older woman with bushy white hair. She wore a Hawaiian shirt and a nametag that read SHIRLEY. When I asked for the harbormaster, she directed me toward the slips near the entrance.

I went out the back, the dock mercifully shaded by a pitched metal roof, and walked past the laundry with its tumbling machines and the pocket grocery store's newspaper stand and hauled up at the end of the pier. Gulls wheeled. Yachts swayed. A boom box balanced on a piling played something by Elvis. Just another day in paradise.

A man in black bathing trunks and flip-flops played a stream of water over one of those sport fishing boats, a top-heavy blue and white job with a narrow hull and a pair of Mercs as big as bike engines. I bet she was fast but prone to capsizing in rough surf.

Watching my approach, the man straightened, shut off the hose and wiped a hand on the back of his trunks. I put him at five-eight and a good two hundred pounds. With thick arms and legs and a chest like the bow of a ship, he looked as if he'd once wrestled in the Olympics.

"Stefan Zelinski?"

"Ah." He gripped my hand. "You are that CW. I recognize your voice. You are friend of Walter Bishop, yes?"

"Yes," I said. "Can I talk to you about the drowning?"

"Drowning?"

"Of Tamika Williams. She died two nights ago at the west end of the pier."

From here, we had a clear line of sight to the condos that lined The Point but the clutter of masts and boats blocked the view of the basin.

"Such a shame. She was young, yes?" He had a deep voice that matched the broad shoulders and chest.

"I understand that the night she died, you rescued a boat that was adrift in the harbor."

"Rescued?"

"Someone borrowed your boat and failed to secure it to the dock."

"Yes, yes. I tell this to police."

"Who do you think took it?"

"I don't know. Someone took it, I don't know. I'm sorry. I cannot care for it."

"You mean you can't get involved."

"Yes, I cannot."

I took a wild guess. "You're afraid you'll be deported."

"In Poland, things are not good now."

"Stefan, I think the person who hurt Tamika Williams did this before. We can't let him get away with it."

He coiled the hose and wiped his hands.

"I just want to know what you saw that night."

"Please. Come to office. I show you what I know."

As soon as we entered his quarters, Shirley said she had to run an errand. Stefan opened a drawer and handed me two documents, a certificate of title and a bill of sale. I'd look at them later. For now, I asked him to explain his movements that night.

Stefan had left the marina a little after 6 p.m. Until then, he'd seen nothing unusual. Since this was the start of the tourist season, the dock and the anchor field were crowded. The yacht owners kept to themselves, but there were always one or two drunk and rowdy people. No one would pay attention to someone diving off a boat, or falling into the water.

Stefan paused the narrative. "How do you say—needle in haystack?"

"Got it in one."

"To see someone from the condominium, yes? You must have eagle eye." He pointed to his.

"What did you tell the police about the boat?"

"Yes. They come and look at boat. It is very clean, scrubbed very clean. They want to know if I touch it. I say, of course I touch, it is my boat. I care for it."

There went that lead.

"It was empty when you found it?" I asked.

"Empty? Yes."

"Banging against the dock."

"Where waves come between the islands, big waves from the storm. Boat is fast but. . . ."

He swayed side to side, a motion that tightened the muscles in his legs.

"But it rocks easily?"

"Yes. It is older boat, for the bay, not the, how do you say?"

"Open water?"

"Yes."

"It's a used boat, yes?"

He nodded.

"Where did you get it?"

"Ha! This is what police want to know."

"And?"

"They are surprised. Maybe you, too."

"Who did you buy it from?"

"My friend, the mayor."

He must have read the look of astonishment that seized my face.

"Yes. Everyone is big surprise."

26.

I GOT MY second shock of the day as I pushed through the doors to Cunningham's office and ran into Officer Charles Stover. Hand braced on his utility belt, he gave me the deadeye stare.

"What you are doing here?"

I returned the look. "I could ask you the same thing."

He lifted an envelope. "Collecting."

"You're a bagman now?"

"For the Police Athletic League. The mayor's our biggest fan."

"I'm sure he is."

Charles glanced over his shoulder at the receptionist, who was working hard to ignore us, and asked, "Am I gonna need to referee this round?"

I raised both hands. "I'm just a taxpayer looking for advice."

"My advice is, let the man do his job."

"How do you know I'm not selling him a house?"

"Cause he already owns most of 'em."

"You can stay if you want."

"I'll be in the car," he said, "in case anyone should need police assistance."

"Just don't drink and drive."

With a nod, he slid through the doorway. I faced the receptionist's desk and produced a business card.

The receptionist did not fit the stereotype. I'd expected a young and buxom woman the mayor could chase around the desk. This one resembled a volunteer at a church supper—gray suit, white top, no jewelry. The knotted hands matched her expression. The plaque on her desk read MARGIE.

"Hello," I said in my cheeriest voice. "I'm here to see the mayor."

"Do you have an appointment?" Margie asked.

Reasonable to a fault.

"A standing one," I said and took a seat.

Although Cunningham had an office at city hall, he maintained this private keep for his appraisal business, atop the same ice-blue high-rise as Charles Palmer. Apparently the only thing separating the tireless promoters of Spanish Point was expensive artwork and a half-mile of tile. Unlike Palmer's quarters, with its plush carpet and exotic wood, Cunningham's digs resembled a dental suite, the pewter walls adorned with abstract collages highlighted in gold leaf. A pile of *Coastal Living* magazines fanned across the table. The flat-screen bolted to the wall showed B-roll footage of the bay.

Lifting the receiver, Margie gurgled into the phone before saying that the mayor would be with me shortly. In the interim, to avoid leafing through the magazines, I stared at my phone and mentally reviewed hizzoner's storied political career.

Phil Cunningham was a strong advocate with strong beliefs. He'd blocked a city initiative to ban assault weapons, supported a crackdown on opioid prescriptions and diverted millions in tax dollars to private business. As for building in flood zones, he maintained that developers could resolve any issue through smart design.

Those private interests had returned the favor. His election to the statehouse was a given, and already there was talk of higher office. One of the state's senators was retiring and rumor had it the governor wanted to send a major donor to Washington. Cunningham looked the part.

The door to the inner sanctum opened and the mayor appeared, looking much like he had the first time we'd met. He wore the slacks to a chalk-stripe suit, a shirt with narrow blue stripes and a red tie adorned with polo players. Flat stomach, boyish face, hair the color of straw. . . . My grandmother would have called him a clotheshorse. But then she'd never known him.

He greeted me with a practiced smile. "To what do I owe the pleasure?"

"I have a few questions."

He spread his hands as if in benediction. "As a public servant, my life is an open book. Ask away."

I'd taken a picture of the license photos of the Venice bombers when Tony had gone to the restroom and asked Cheryl to check the men with the mayor's charity. Both Skulls and Bottlenose had been part of Suncoast Generations, the program for wayward youth. Voice lowered, my back to the receptionist, I produced the phone and showed the images to Cunningham.

"Do you know these two?"

He took the phone, his expression of mild interest unchanged.

"Who are they?"

"They're the pair who rammed my bike and sent a friend through a window."

"I'm sorry to hear. Is your friend all right?"

"No thanks to these two. I understand they're graduates of your program."

"If you mean Suncoast, we've helped a lot of troubled youth. But if you're asking if I know them, no, I'm not hands-on with the program anymore."

Unless you want a ready source of muscle, I thought but kept that to myself.

"Then you didn't send them after me."

Returning the phone, he chuckled. "If I want to stop you from doing something, I'll use the courts—as you know." He smiled, revealing perfect teeth in a perfect white.

"Touché."

"Speaking of trouble." He pointed to the television and images of a crew affixing what looked like a giant stethoscope to one of InSpire's walls. "I assume that's your handiwork?"

"No, but you could consider it a public service."

"You could consider it economic suicide."

"Do I hear a threat?"

He waved an arm toward his office. "I'm forgetting my manners. Come in, have a seat. Can I get you something to drink?"

The receptionist looked from her computer and something passed between them. Maybe a signal that, if he yelled for help, she was to call Officer Stover.

I said thank you, no. He closed the door and walked behind the desk but did not sit. Neither did I, choosing to stare across the Trail to the marina.

"Nice view," I said.

"We like it."

"You can see the place where Tamika Williams washed ashore."

Turning from the window, I watched his mouth tighten, the first sign I'd gotten to him. Our eyes locked. The silence stretched. The phone rang. He answered and told the caller to wait, he wouldn't be long.

He turned. "You have no legal standing here, but since you're a colleague of my wife's, as a professional courtesy I can give you two minutes. Go."

"Did you falsify the geotechnical report on Vertex?"

"No."

"Did you manipulate the stock of Thompson Partners?"

He crossed his arms. "No."

"Did you have anything to do with the death of Ryan Donovan?"

"No. Next question."

"Did you have anything to do with the death of Tamika Williams?"

"You're starting to sound like a broken record."

"I could say the same of you."

He squeezed his mouth. "The night she died, I was the guest of honor at a fundraiser, at the home of our mutual friend, Charles Palmer. You can check with him, or the police."

That revelation shouldn't have come as a surprise but it did.

"Tamika fell, or was pushed, from your boat."

Lines clotted his forehead. "It's not my boat, and that's not what the official report says."

As nominal head of the police department, he would have access, damn him. I found the photo of the bill of sale and handed the phone to him.

He glanced at the image. "You just proved my point."

"The harbormaster lets you borrow the boat to take your buddies fishing."

"Anyone with a license and life vest can borrow it."

"Why did you sell the boat?"

"I don't have a lot of time to fish," he said. "Unlike some people."

I took his meaning but couldn't stop. "What do you have on Stefan?"

He chuckled. "I don't have anything on Stefan. I'm his sponsor, if that's what you mean."

Retrieving a messenger bag from a chair, he removed a document and held it in front of my face. I read the heading: Affidavit of Support under Section 213A of the Act, Department of Homeland Security, U.S. Citizenship and Immigration Services. The paper listed Stefan Zelinski as the petitioner and Philip Cunningham as financial guarantor.

"I imagine Stefan would do anything for his sponsor," I said. "Like cleaning your boat."

He slid the form into the bag and straightened. "He's fastidious."

"And loyal."

"We're on the same side, you know."

"What side is that?"

"We make it possible for people to live anywhere they want. This country, this city, these islands." He moved toward the door. "It's their choice. Not some government entity telling them what they can and can't do, with themselves or their property. That right ranks up there with life, liberty and the pursuit of happiness."

"I understand the concept. What I don't understand is how we can put people in harm's way and justify the profits."

He raised his hands as if giving a sermon. "It's called progress, Ms. McCoy, and we've been doing it this way for the last 240 years. Grow big or go home."

"Catchy."

"Threads make the man, slogans make a campaign. You should try it."

"What, run for office?"

He crossed in front of me, so close I could sense the body heat and the faintly bitter scent of cologne, and touched the handle of the door. "You'd be good. You're aggressive, and direct. You have friends in the department. You'd have to watch your associates, though. What you rub up against rubs off on you."

Cunningham had stepped into my space but I refused to retreat. I had a good two inches on him, one of the advantages of stature. I took a breath, the air so thick it stuck in my throat, and leaned in, to make absolutely certain he heard me. "Is that another threat?"

"Consider it a word to the wise." His tight grin displayed no teeth, only the confident menace of the bully. With his connections, he had to know who organized the opposition to Vertex. And he had to know who'd called the media. Maybe the accident wasn't road rage. And maybe I hadn't been the only target.

I had people to warn.

27.

I LEFT IN a dark cloud of anger. Walking to the office, I stuffed the buds in my ears and listened to Luke Combs sing "She Got the Best of Me." When it came to the mayor, I hadn't come close. I'd manage to aggravate one of the most powerful persons on the Gulf Coast and had nothing to show, except the sick feeling that I'd endangered my friends. All I knew was that word of my performance would reach Casey and she would demand a reckoning.

Not wanting to repeat yesterday's challenge from an oversized vehicle, I took the alley behind the opera house to Main Street and stopped at the traffic circle that fronted our office. Melissa stood beside the model of the 19th century schooner. She had a sour expression and a cell phone glued to her ear. Maybe she was having men trouble. Maybe she was pregnant. I'd heard that could mess with your hormones.

Not wanting to interrupt her conversation, I raised my hand in passing when I heard an engine rev and turned to watch a Jeep careen through the roundabout and aim for us.

"Melissa!" I yelled and tackled her waist.

We hit the grass strip between street and sidewalk and rolled as the Jeep plowed the schooner through the office wall, the air bursting with metal, glass and wood.

"You all right?" I yelled and, when she nodded, rose to confront the driver.

The impact had blown parts of the schooner sideways, littering the sidewalk with hunks of wood. The Jeep coughed and died and in the silence, Bottlenose slid from the vehicle, a hand covering a bloody face. Spotting me, he made a run for the roundabout. Grabbing a mast from the shattered boat, I made a left-handed swing to connect with the back of his head. He went facedown onto the flowers that decorated the circle and lay there.

Rising from the median, Melissa presented scrapes on both arms and legs but her limbs still worked. The office hadn't fared as well. Half in, half out of the building, the Jeep had buckled the window frames and shattered the wall that displayed our most expensive homes—our signature properties, as Casey liked to say. The vehicle looked familiar. It wasn't the one that had crashed into Rae and me, but the damage to the left front bumper suggested it might be the one that had tried to clip me near the marina. As sirens stretched the air, I crunched over broken glass to check for injuries. No one sat at the reception desk but the lobby had filled as people detoured around the debris to reach the sidewalk.

"Everyone OK?" I yelled and got a few verbals and a number of nods. Elaine from New York tried to pick her way around the heaps of canvas and wood. I helped her to the curb as the first responders arrived, the beat cops in their blue-and-whites, then the reinforcements—Cheryl and Charles Stover and the blonde officer from the marina the night Tamika had died. The blonde took charge, backing us away from the intersection while calling for Cheryl and Stover to secure the scene.

Agents streamed from the office, many rounding the building from the entrance in back. I was heading for the lobby to search for Casey and anyone in the conference rooms when she appeared, motioning with both hands as if urging a flock of sheep into the pasture.

"We all out?" I asked.

Her jaw hardened. "Where is the idiot who did this?" Pointing to the body in the circle now surrounded by uniforms she asked, "Who is that?"

"He's the idiot." Only when extending the shard of mast did I realize I was still holding it.

The vein in Casey's temple ticked like a clock. "What in God's name does he think he's doing?"

I wanted to say *resting* but held my tongue.

Casey surveyed the roof—it hadn't collapsed—and wondered aloud whether the damage would discourage our clients. "Not to mention the publicity," she said as a TV news van stopped half-a-block from the intersection.

I suggested that saving the agents from injury might be the upside here.

A red Fire/Rescue truck blocked the circle. A man and a woman in blazing white shirts piled bags on a gurney and pushed it toward Bottlenose. Gently, they rolled him onto his back, trailed a light across his eyes, secured his neck with a brace and transferred him to the gurney. Then, with a jerk to shake loose the struts, they wheeled him to the ambulance.

Casey watched with stoic pessimism. "I have to admit, you are very cool in a crisis."

"Glad to be of service."

"I hope this isn't related to any of your extracurricular activities."

I'd been wondering that myself but didn't have time to finish the thought.

"While I appreciate your heroics, there is the matter of the meeting you had this morning with the mayor. You confronted Phil about the death of Tamika Williams.

"I had some questions."

"Apparently you accused him of murder."

"Is he going to press charges?"

Buckled across her chest, her arms reminded me of a straightjacket. "I'd like to think he's above that."

I couldn't agree, but Cunningham did present a danger. He'd already filed one order to keep me from encroaching on his personal space. And he could afford better lawyers than I could, starting with Mitch's father.

Casey cleared her throat. "I thought we agreed that you would post your schedule with Melissa."

Melissa had retreated to a low wall. Had it extended to the corner, it would have stopped the vehicle as effectively as a line of posts. But that would have blocked the view of the office.

I tapped my thigh with the oversized stick. "Maybe I could wear an ankle monitor."

"There is no need to be sarcastic."

Melissa bent forward and pressed the heels of her hands to her forehead.

"I think your daughter could use some help," I said, as much to render aid as to redirect Casey. She glared and headed in the opposite direction, toward Leslie Roberts and her TV crew.

Cheryl stepped into the vacuum. She pointed to my side. "That what you used to subdue him?"

The mast resembled a splintered baseball bat. I'd gripped it so hard my hand bled.

Cheryl snapped on a pair of translucent gloves. "You wanna give me that?"

I handed her the stick.

"You OK? I can call EMS."

I shook my head.

"I've got a first aid kit in the car. Wait here."

I stared at the Jeep, its nose buried in the wall. "I'm fine."

She motioned to one of the patrol officers to take the shard, gave me a handkerchief and extracted a notebook from a back pocket. "You always did walk softly."

I smiled at the allusion. Despite her stern exterior, Officer Finzi was a lot kinder that I'd been in my day.

Her voice brought me back. "You wanna tell me what happened?"

I did, omitting the part about the mayor. That thought led to a much darker one. "What I'd like to know is how'd this guy tracked me down?"

"You don't watch the news, do you? You're all over the air, the woman who saved Venice from the mad bombers."

"Who leaked that?"

Cheryl aimed her chin across the intersection, where Casey huddled with Roberts and her crew. "Your buddy, Miss Action News. She's all over it."

"How?"

"She spotted you at the bombers' house."

"I don't remember seeing a news crew, but then I might have been busy ducking for cover."

"I can just hear it," Cheryl said. 'Hey, isn't that the chick who tried to drive her bike through the restaurant?'"

"That's an exaggeration."

"They feed off this stuff. It's like mother's milk."

"That blows my cover with Casey."

Cheryl glanced at my boss, whose frown made her chin resemble a shovel. "Like you ever had one."

"Listen," I said. "Are we done here? I'm supposed to meet Tony at noon."

"You gonna unload on him?" She pointed to the handkerchief wrapped around my palm. "Show him your battle scars?"

Straightening, I said I might.

"I'd like to see his face."

I swept an arm to indicate the field of debris. "There is no way I'm to blame for this."

"Hey," she said. "People who live in glass houses. . . ."

28.

DRIVING NORTH TOWARD Rae's bar, I fumed over yet another attempt by the Dynamic Duo to grind me into grout. I'd told Cheryl that I was fine. Truth told, I wasn't. My stomach clenched and my batting arm still shook. Worst of all, I didn't feel safe.

And then there was the encounter with the mayor. I could handle street crime. It was the white-color variety that left me feeling helpless.

I kept scanning the rearview mirrors and tensing for the ambush. Which was irrational, since the police had both of my attackers in custody.

The crash was yet another screw-up in a week of them. Two people were dead. The investigation had stalled. The market had smoked my 401(k). And although I should have known better, the mayor hadn't rolled over. He hadn't even budged.

Then there was the job. Selling real estate was hard enough without getting in my own way. If inspectors found cracks at InSpire, the towers were toast. The city might put Vertex on hold. Casey would look for someone to blame. Judging by her comments to date, my time at Laine & Company was limited, perhaps my career as well.

Anger turned to paranoia and paranoia morphed into defeat. I was struck dumb by a sense of futility, convinced that, however hard I worked, I would never discover the truth, or find someone to help.

The one bright spot remained the promise of seeing Walter glide into the marina, and even that felt spoiled by the radio— Randy Houser singing about running out of moonlight. He was right. Everything had its season. Time, patience, romance—they were all finite. I'd pressed Mitch hard about his firm's role in the mayor's stock scam. The same with Tony and the probe into Tamika's death. Both were forgiving but there were limits, and I might have pushed them to theirs.

Kicking those questions down the road, I switched the station to NPR and caught an update on the stock market. It had taken another leg down, led by shares of national homebuilders with exposure to Florida. The stock of Thompson Partners had suffered the biggest drop. Trading had been halted.

Avoiding the traffic on the Tamiami Trail allowed me to bypass the towers. I didn't need to see inspectors and survey crews crawling over InSpire, or an angry Dean Caldwell, who like Casey would be looking for someone to blame.

I arrived at Cirque a little after noon, crunching over a shell-covered parking lot suspiciously devoid of cars. As I rounded the corner by the bay, the hole in the south wall of the restaurant told me why.

The interior looked as if a hurricane had hit. Rae stood in the middle of the room with an inverted chair between her knees, using her cast to hammer its legs into place. A cook and a couple of wait staff used shovels and brooms to push splintered furniture toward the entrance.

Without looking Rae yelled, "We're closed!"

Spider cracks radiated from the mirror behind the bar. Light pierced the hole in the wall and glinted from the spray of glass that covered the floor. "No kidding."

Rae met my eyes. "You missed all the excitement."

I sidestepped a puddle of beer that leaked from a pile of longnecks. "What happened?"

She puffed air to dislodge a strand of hair that had wandered into her eye. When that didn't work, she used the cast to clear her forehead. "Vandals, that's what happened."

"Does Eddie know about it?"

"I haven't told him yet."

"How's he doing?"

"Eddie? Awful. He looks like a stone."

"How are you doing?"

Rae looked at the chair as if it had just appeared. "I couldn't decide whether to cry or collapse, so I came to work, to get away from it all." Using the cast, she pointed to the handkerchief still wrapped around my fingers. "What'd you do to the hand?"

I told her about the fight with Bottlenose.

"Geeze, trouble follows you everywhere. I told you not to piss those guys off."

The wait staff had cleared the deck of debris and started to move the undamaged tables. With Rae on one end and me on the other, we dragged one of the four-tops to the center of the room.

"What if it's more than that?" I asked.

"More than what?"

I told her about my theory of Cunningham—that he'd tried to bury the subsidence report and, when it became public, profit from the fallout.

"You think the most powerful guy on the west coast hired a bunch of thugs to take us out?" She snorted. "Your problem is that you're jonesing for this guy. Next thing you'll blame him for Korean nukes and the war in the Middle East."

We dragged the last of the furniture into place. "Cunningham said he knew who'd been organizing the protests and feeding me information. What if you were the target?"

"Why?" She sidestepped the staff as they set the tables. "So the city can demolish this place quicker and build a bigger dock?"

"Your nephew was a whistleblower. People might assume he talked to you and Eddie."

"The cracks and sinkholes? It's all over the TV."

"But your testimony might link Ryan and the report to the death of Tamika Williams. That's not public."

The cook hauled a pair of garbage bags to the promenade. "Hey!" Rae yelled. "Keep 'em off the walk."

"You need to look after yourselves," I said.

"Not my first rodeo, kiddo."

"And I wouldn't be so visible at these protests."

She grinned. "Bad news travels fast."

The lights snapped on.

"It's not all bad," I said. "Walter's coming back."

"When?"

"Sometime tomorrow."

Grabbing a rag, she began sweeping glass from the bar top. "You need moral support?"

"You don't have to work?"

She spread her hands. "How busy you think we'll be?"

I said I'd appreciate the company.

"Jerry," Rae yelled. "Get a broom and take care of this mess." She stopped mopping the bar. "What'd you say about a source?"

"The mayor thinks I have an inside source on the Tamika Williams investigation."

"Like that weird little man you're hanging out with."

"His name is Hud and we're not hanging out. He works for a ride-share company and gave me a lift after Skulls hit the bike."

"He follows you like a puppy."

"He likes to pretend he's my CI. How do you hear this stuff?"

From the floor, Rae retrieved a bottle of vodka and slapped it on the counter. "Don't these jerks know how much this stuff costs?"

"Rae?"

"He's stopped by a couple of times looking for you."

"What'd he say?"

"He wanted to talk to you about a necklace."

I felt my blood freeze.

Tony Delgado chose that moment to walk through the opening that fronted the bay.

Rae gave him a nod. "I'd say you're the one who needs to look after herself."

29.

HANDS ON HIPS, Tony surveyed the damage. "You call this in?"

"The cops were already here," Rae said. "The tall blonde with arms like a sledge hammer. Looks like she works out with the Lakers." She pointed her cast at me. "Try it sometime. It'll help when you take down the bad guys."

Tony stood in silhouette but I could see his eyebrows knot. "What about the bad guys?"

"She'll tell you all about it."

"Thanks," I said.

"Anytime," she said. "Detective, you here for lunch?"

"I think lunch is off," I told Tony.

The cook peeked from the shattered door to the kitchen.

"Jerry," Rae yelled. "Anything working back there besides the lights?"

'Fridge and grill," he said. "That's about it."

"Fire it up and give us a couple of dogs." She turned to us. "On the house. Can't let a couple of troupers like you go hungry. That OK?"

We mumbled our thanks.

"You want something to drink while you wait?"

"Water," we said at the same time.

"Have a seat," Rae said and swept glass from the bar. "You want catsup and mustard? Relish should still be good. Fries will have to wait."

A man hollered. Rae disappeared into the kitchen to emerge with two hotdogs in paper boats and two bottles of water already slick with moisture. Tony offered to pay but she raised her hands and told us to grab some napkins from one of the tables. Emerging into sunshine and the smell of water, we ate lunch while strolling the concrete ribbon along the bay.

"Just think," I said, trying to keep mustard from my shirt. "If the Scots who settled here had hung onto this land, how much they'd be worth."

"In case you hadn't noticed, I'm not a Scot."

"Say you were."

He dabbed his lips. "I suppose this is your version of 'someday all this will be yours.'"

"Someday all this will be under water, or one giant sinkhole, depending on who you believe."

"That's what's bothering you?"

"Who said anything's bothering me?"

His eyes were the color of coffee. They roamed my face. "You've got that look."

"What look?"

"That look where your eyebrows come together and you squint, as if you're trying to see something no one else can see."

"Is that all you've got?"

"And you pout."

I took another bite of the hotdog. "I do not pout."

"It's cute."

"Cute is for Barbie. I don't do cute."

"How about endearing?"

His stare sent goosebumps down my arms. Until now, Tony had never said anything even remotely romantic.

"I heard about the attack at your office," he said. "That how you hurt your hand?"

"I wasn't wearing my batting gloves."

"You might have left it to us. You're getting quite the reputation."

We stopped at the end of Baywalk. Avoiding his eyes, I looked over the Intracoastal toward the bridge to the keys.

"He would have gotten away," I said. "Both of them."

"That seems to be your new theme. You want to tell me what's going on?"

"I suppose you'll find out eventually." I told him about my disastrous meeting with the mayor and why I'd confronted him in the first place.

"I'm listening," Tony said. "Make the case."

"OK. Here's the theory. Cunningham is heavily invested, financially and politically, in Vertex. He stands to lose a fortune if the project is scuttled because of subsidence. I don't know if he had anything to do with the death or Ryan Donovan, but his fingerprints are all over Tamika."

"We didn't find his prints anywhere."

"Would you just listen?"

The towers of InSpire hove into view, the one a great icicle poking the sky, the other a bed of concrete and steel clawing the air. I couldn't stand still, so I turned back toward the bar. Good sport that he was, Tony followed.

"OK," I said. "What if Tamika approached him with the idea that they open an investigation into Ryan's report? Cunningham can blow off a newbie with a testing firm but she runs the planning department. She's a threat. What if he told her to meet him at the marina because the boat ride would give them some privacy?"

"That's a lot of ifs."

"There's more. What if they plow through the pass on their way to the Gulf and the water's still rough from the storm? She goes overboard—he dumps her or she falls—and he comes back to the marina and forgets to tie up the boat. Stefan the harbormaster gets the call and you discover the body."

"The mayor sold the boat."

"Stefan says anyone could use it anytime they wanted."

"The mayor's got an alibi. We're waiting for the tox report on Williams but door-to-door came up empty, and the boat looks like it just rolled out of the factory."

"What about phone records? Who called Tamika the day she died?"

"A dozen people, including someone from your agency."

That caught me. "Who?"

"We're still checking."

We headed north, the waves from boat wakes slapping the spine of riprap as if it were an old friend. "You knew from the harbormaster that Cunningham had owned the boat and that he had an alibi and you didn't tell me."

"You're not part of the investigation. If you want to go back to school. . . ."

"You know I won't carry a gun." Or face my demons, he could have said but didn't. I liked him for that. "So I guess I'm on my own."

"We'll handle it."

"In the meantime, I've tried to save a drowning man, had an encounter with a glass wall not once but twice and can't do my job because inspectors are crawling over InSpire like it's a jungle gym."

"How did the TV station find out about the towers?"

I waved the napkin and hotdog boat. "I didn't call them."

"Who did?"

"I can't say."

"Can't or won't."

"Even if I told you, you wouldn't believe it."

He shook his head. "So you have your own network of informants now."

"I wouldn't call it a network."

"Be careful, especially with the mayor."

"I can take care of myself."

Tony raised a hand but didn't break stride. "You know I can't protect you."

"I'm not asking you to."

"Technically, the mayor's our boss."

"Technically, he's responsible for two, maybe three deaths if we can nail him for Susan Thompson, not to mention a giant trading scheme that could cost the city millions."

"Have you shared any of this with your boss?"

"Casey? Not directly."

"I'd be careful about what you say."

"You mean because she's my employer."

"I mean because she's still married to Cunningham."

Rae's bar hove into view. Dabbing his lips, Tony crumpled the napkin and paper boat and held out a hand for mine. For the first time that afternoon he smiled. "You want a real lunch?"

"No, thanks. I'm good." I smiled and took a beat to relish the feeling, hoping against hope it would last.

30.

"IT'S A WEEK since the storm and there's water in your front yard," I said when Cheryl met me at the door of her house.

"Look who's talking." She took the proffered bottle of wine and pointed next door to the home I'd inherited from my grandfather. "Yours looks like a swamp."

"It is a swamp."

We stood on the stoop of her block-and-stucco one-story with its wild bougainvillea and concrete drive and watched palm fronds float down the gutter. It wasn't just the big storms that flooded the coast. During high tide, water from the Intracoastal backed into the storm sewers and overran the yards.

"Where's it gonna go?" she asked.

"Back in the air," I said.

"So why are we standing out here?"

"Good point," I said and held the door.

The interior looked similar to Pap's house. The combination living/dining room sported a single window. The kitchen had a pillar to support the ceiling. The floor was vinyl parquet, the cabinets laminate over particleboard. Those things hadn't stopped Cheryl from brightening the place with pictures her daughter had drawn.

Sugar Bear loped across the floor, nails ticking, her head cocked as if asking for ID. I bent to scratch her ear when Tracy bounded down the hallway.

"Aunt Candace!" she shrieked.

"Indoor voice, please!" Cheryl said and headed for the kitchen.

I gave my goddaughter a hug. She was tall for her age, with brown hair to her waist and green eyes like her mother.

"You wanna see this new game I got?" She lifted a shining face and her smartphone.

"Hey," Cheryl said. "Don't you have homework?"

"Mom, it's the weekend."

"Always an excuse."

Tracy ran down the hall and disappeared.

"Happy girl," I said.

Cheryl uncorked the wine, pinched two glasses between her fingers and, with a jerk of her head, motioned toward the patio in back. "Give her a few years."

Once outside, she plopped down at a glass-topped table we'd found at a consignment shop and looked at me with smudged eyes. "So how you doing?"

"I've had better days."

"Haven't we all."

She poured. We drank and listened to the traffic noise. Light bleeding from the city blurred the stars.

"How's the hand?"

I flexed it. It hurt about the same as my leg. "Serviceable. What's the latest on Bottlenose?"

"No concussion, if that's what you're worried about. He's in general population with his buddy."

"Bail?"

"With all those bombs and guns? Those two'll grow mold before they see daylight."

I poured more wine. "You think they're working for the mayor?"

"Doing what? Parking cars at his campaign rallies?"

"Keeping Rae and me from following up on the geotech report?"

Cheryl drained her glass and refilled. "Why in God's name would Phil Cunningham have Tamika Williams killed?"

"Because if Tamika pressed for an investigation, it would derail the project and the stock would tank."

"The stock already tanked."

"She died before the possibility of sinkholes became public knowledge."

"So he tried to keep her quiet, is what you're saying?"

"And when that failed, he covered his position by shorting the stock. No matter what happens to Vertex, he wins."

"And risk life in jail for a few more bucks? You don't know the ruling class."

"I know he's a political animal and will do anything to stay on top."

"OK," Cheryl said. "Who's got the proof?"

"Mitch."

"Mitch Palmer? He ain't gonna testify against his father, even if you've got him twisted around your finger. Sell out Cunningham to save the family business, yeah, I'll buy that. But turn on his dad? Uh-uh. No way."

"What about Ryan Donovan? How do you explain his death?"

"He went surfing during a hurricane. What did he expect?"

I filled her in on what Melissa had told me about their fight.

Cheryl topped our glasses. "Why'd she tell you that?

"Guilt, I think."

"A lot of that going around these days."

I raised my brows and felt better that the motion no longer hurt. "You have anyone in mind?"

"You."

"Me?"

"I'm just saying, you can't fix everything."

I was not going to let her wild supposition interfere with my theory. "Let's get back to the case. So the ME thinks Ryan's death was an accident. What about Tamika?"

"The jury's still out."

"I hear you guys came up empty on the door-to-door."

"You've really gotta press this, don't you?"

I said I did.

"OK," Cheryl said. "We've got one witness, an old guy on one of the yachts, glasses thick as this." She raised the wine bottle and confirmed its empty state. "You want to crack open another?"

I shook my head. It hadn't started to swim and I wanted to keep it that way. "What'd the guy say?"

"He said he saw a tall man wearing a baseball cap running from a fishing boat."

"So it could have been the mayor."

"It ain't the mayor."

"What if the stock swindle. . . ."

"It ain't a swindle."

"What if the stock trade is Phil getting back at Tommy Thompson for accusing him of killing his wife."

"You say that out loud," Cheryl said, "and you'll be the one going to jail."

The image of the Jeep crashing into the office returned with clarity. "It might be safer than going to work."

"How come you're not pumping the dashing detective for all this?"

I hesitated.

Cheryl's smile lit the patio. "Because you finally did the deed?"

I thought the skin would peel from my cheeks. "Because things are better."

"Better? That's the best you can do?"

"I try to stay out of his face and he tries not to arrest me."

"Good arrangement."

I told her about Rae's bar—she'd already heard about it—and hotdogs along the promenade.

"Sounds romantic. At least one of us might get lucky."

"Lucky isn't the word I'd choose."

"Then why'd you put all of that foo-foo crap in your hair?"

"The highlights?" I asked.

"Yeah. You look like what's-her-name, that woman you used to work for."

"My broker, Mary Margaret?"

"Yeah. Didn't Mitch Palmer hook up with her after you threw him over?"

"Be honest," I said. "You think I'm still after him?"

"It's pretty obvious, isn't it?"

I tipped my head and stared at the scrum of clouds obscuring the stars. "You're going to tell me whether I ask or not, so I might as well ask. What's so obvious?"

"Why you're chasing Mitch and not Tony."

"Why?"

"Because he's everything you're not."

I wasn't following. "Not what?"

"A cop."

"Ouch."

"You wanted honest," she said.

"Couldn't you lie for a change?"

"We've had too much of that."

"All right," I said. "Since we're being honest, what's the deal with Charles Stover?"

Cheryl addressed herself to the empty glass. "We date, every now and then. It's no big deal."

"That night at the hospital, he looked edgy."

"It was a BAC test, not a pap smear. Maybe he thought you'd cut up rough—not like that's ever happened."

"I'm not talking about my blood alcohol content." I told her that during the traffic stop, Stover had warned me against investigating Tamika's death.

"That's nothing."

"What do you mean, 'that's nothing'?"

"They knew each other from way back. I hear they went to Howard the same time. Grew up in a city that didn't care if they grew up at all. He's been looking out for her ever since."

As if someone had thrown a switch, my anger vanished.

Cheryl said, "He feels guilty he couldn't protect her."

"She wouldn't have gotten on that boat if I hadn't dumped this mess in her lap."

"You don't know that."

"What about the other screw-ups on my watch? I drove Walter who-knows-where. I failed to rescue Ryan. I could've gotten Rae killed, or half the people in the office—at least the front half."

"If I'd known we were gonna have a pity party, I would've sent out invitations."

"Too much drama?" I asked.

"Jesus take the wheel."

"What's that supposed to mean?"

"It means you need more help than I can give you."

"Thanks," I said.

"Don't mention it."

"I won't."

"Feel better?"

"Oddly enough, yes."

"You know what your problem is?" Cheryl said. "You try too hard."

"As opposed to not giving a shit?"

"What's that poem about trying to change things you can't?"

"You mean the Serenity Prayer," I said.

"You've heard of it."

"Walter taught it to me," I said.

"Maybe you should listen to him."

I thought of blurting 'if I could find him' but my heart ached enough, so in a quiet voice I said, "Maybe I should."

For a woman with her own troubles, Cheryl could get pretty smug. Before sadness morphed into resentment I pleaded exhaustion and offered to bus the table.

Cheryl waved me into the house and, nudging the door with her foot, said, "You're like that guy who tilted at windmills. Always trying to fix everybody and everything. What's gonna happen if you keep pressing the mayor? You think he'll roll over and play dead? The guy's on the way up. He makes the statehouse and it's a hop, skip and a jump to DC."

Setting the bottle and glasses in the sink, she led me to the front door and flicked the switch for the outside light. We would finish the conversation where it started, on the front stoop, as the water ran a brownish-purple under the streetlights.

My phone buzzed. I knew Cheryl would ask if the message was from Tony or Mitch so I told her the text was from Hud and that he wanted to meet. "He says he knows who did it, whatever that means."

"Now?" she asked, propping the door with a foot. "It's dark."

"It's not a school night."

"Where does this clown want to meet?"

"Does it matter?" I asked.

"I wanna know where to find the body."

"His or mine?"

"Cute."

"You know the county park east of I-75?" I said. "The one with two lakes?"

"The one with alligators in every ditch?"

"That's the one," I said. "Where a normal state would put shoulders."

"I thought you didn't like that neighborhood."

"I just don't like showing homes there." It was too dark, too deserted, with too many overgrown mobile homes fenced in with chicken wire. Just the kind of place Hud would choose to maintain his cloak of secrecy.

Cheryl seemed to read my mind. "This sound right to you?"

It didn't, but I felt an obligation to go, and convincing Cheryl that things were OK was a first step toward convincing myself. "I'll admit, it's a bit theatrical."

"What's this guy playing, secret agent? You wanna be careful. This isn't the little retirement village it was thirty years ago."

"He's harmless."

"If I had a nickel for every time I've heard that."

"You could always loan me your Glock," I said.

"Are you out of your freakin' mind?"

"It's a joke," I said. "You know how I feel about guns."

"You don't need a gun. What you need is common sense."

"It's probably nothing."

"You think he's blowing smoke?" Cheryl asked.

"He wants to take down Cunningham as much as I do."

"He wants to be a hero and doesn't care who he takes down."

I'd considered heading home but Cheryl's rectitude bothered me. What if Hud had stumbled onto valuable information? What if he'd put himself at risk to get it? As sketchy as his intel had been so far, it could provide my only lead.

"You want a wingman?" Cheryl asked.

I stepped from the stoop. "I'll be fine."

"Famous last words," she said and closed the door.

31.

EAST OF THE interstate, the city dissolved into primordial wilderness, the land thick with palmetto and palm. Stomach churning, I drove faster than needed, peeling off the highway with a screech of tires. The access road ran through a dark hammock of pine. Waterlogged ditches cut through the berms on both sides. There were a few streetlamps but half weren't lit. Rounding a bend, my headlights picked out another vehicle, large and black, an Escalade or some other monster SUV, its right front tire sinking toward a drainage ditch. The car had stopped but the lights were on. Slowing, I spotted a figure standing near the driver's side, and the back of another vehicle. A red Prius.

There was no debris and, judging from the rear of the Toyota, no sign of a collision. Yet the scene had traffic accident written all over it. Pulling over as far as I could, I left the lights burning, grabbed my phone and stepped from the car.

The road was quiet, the muted sound of interstate traffic filtering through the woods. An easterly wind had risen to chase the clouds across the moon. Closing on the SUV, I recognized Casey Laine. She stood with back bowed and arms folded around her chest as if she were freezing.

"Are you all right?" I yelled and closed the distance. "Is anybody hurt?"

She stared in the direction of the Prius. It wasn't until I pulled even with the front of the SUV that I saw the body. It was Hud. He lay on his side, legs crumpled, one hand flung over his head as if he were flagging a ride. His crutches littered the pavement. It looked like a hit and run but there were no skid marks, and no corroborating evidence from traffic cams.

He looked uncomfortable, his limbs at all the wrong angles, but I resisted the urge to straighten them. Crouching by the body, I checked for a pulse and found none. A deep chill swept through my core. Calculating the angle of the SUV and the distance between it and the body, I became aware of a person in the weeds by the side of the road. She was doubled over but even as darkness shrouded half her body I recognized Melissa Cunningham.

In the distance, sirens wailed. I pulled my phone and called Emergency Operations and learned that officers and EMS were on the way. Rising, I walked to Casey. She leaned against the driver's door of the SUV, a company car placarded with the Laine & Company schooner, and tracked my approach with heavy eyes.

As the sirens morphed into a pair of Florida Highway Patrol cruisers, she told Melissa to pull herself together and get in the car. Arms buckled around her knees, Melissa ignored the order.

The two black-and-browns stopped well away from the other vehicles and angled their lights at the body. The first FHP officer, a tall, thin man in a gray-brown uniform and Smokey the Bear hat, shone a Maglite on me and asked if I were involved. His nametag said Robinson. I said I'd just arrived and stopped to offer assistance. The second officer, short and dark with a tag that said Hicks, bent near Hud's body but played his eyes over Casey and Melissa. Returning to his car, he stuck his hand through the open window, grabbed a microphone and called for a second Fire/Rescue truck and the coroner.

Approaching Casey, Robinson asked for ID and, once he'd check it, asked if she wouldn't mind telling him what had happened. Hicks did the same with Melissa, who remained on the ground and spoke without raising her head. I knew that, once they figured it out, the politeness would turn clinical, but for now, the troopers sounded as if they were asking for directions.

Casey said she'd rounded the corner and felt something hit the car. She'd thought it was an animal. It was dark and she hadn't seen anyone in the road. She spoke with the patience of someone explaining the obvious. Calm, maybe too calm, although it could have been shock. Melissa cinched her arms around her legs and buried her head, the raven hair spilling over her knees.

It all felt wrong. I took another look at the position of the vehicles. Whoever rode on the passenger side would have stepped into part of the retention ditch while climbing from the vehicle. Melissa's shoes and capris were dry. Casey's capris looked damp, and a spatter of mud clung to her ankles and shoes.

Casey saw me looking. She must have guessed I'd put it together and, as Trooper Robinson returned to his cruiser, summoned me with the tilt of her head.

I faced her. "Which one of you hit him?"

She watched the troopers cordon the area. "Does it matter?"

"Why don't you walk me through it, starting with Ryan Donovan."

"That was an accident. He was another one of Melissa's 'friends.'" She used air quotes for the word *friends*. "One of those daredevils who likes to do stupidly dangerous things."

"So his death has no connection with the effort to cover up the test results."

"Happenstance, as my mother used to say. Although it did catch your eye, more's the pity."

"Melissa turned back but the gatehouse has no record of you coming or going that night."

She managed a grim smile. "With my husband, if you must know."

I took a not-so-wild guess. "But you were really with Tommy Thompson."

Arms folded, she stared at the police, her face brittle in the strobing light.

"Payback?" I asked.

"I always get my man."

"That's the first time I've heard you tell a joke."

She met my eyes. "The boy drowned. Let's leave it at that."

We were getting sidetracked. I asked her about Tamika Williams.

"That was a misunderstanding."

"The woman died," I said. "I'd hardly call that a misunderstanding."

"I'd called her about an unrelated matter. She expressed concern about a rumor she'd heard and wondered whether the city should order an inspection. We tried to impress on her the damage that would do to the project and the city's bond rating. When she asked to see the agency's report on the project, we invited her on a tour, to give her some perspective."

"From the water."

"You know how the press hounds us. This offered some privacy."

"And when you couldn't convince her of your position, you pushed her in."

"She'd discovered Melissa's connection with the Donovan boy and wouldn't let it go. We tried to explain that Melissa wasn't there when he drowned but Ms. Williams became exercised. She started accusing Melissa of conspiring to defraud the city and they got into a tussle."

"And Melissa pushed her."

"She fell. It was an accident."

"But Melissa let her drown."

"That was unfortunate."

"Was Cunningham involved?"

"What is this obsession you have with Phil? He'll soon be available, if that's what you'd like."

"I'd like the truth."

"He had no idea we were meeting Ms. Williams. It's one of the few awful things he hasn't done."

"What happened to the boat?"

"Don't you mean what happened to the fingerprints and blood?" She snorted. "We called the harbormaster, anonymously, of course, and he took care of it. A fastidious man, although I doubt he suspected anything."

"Her necklace went missing."

"Melissa grabbed it, to keep Ms. Williams from falling. It's at the bottom of the bay, if you'd like to look for it."

The road seemed to ignite with sound and light as the photographer, crime-scene techs and ambulance crew arrived. They swarmed the body, blocking our view.

"What about Gary Hudson?" I asked. "Were you planning to put him at the bottom of the bay?"

"That man was an animal. He was stalking Melissa, calling her, following her, confronting her with these wild accusations that she'd murdered both of those people."

"Did he want money to keep quiet?"

"Oh, no." Her voice broke. "He wanted something far more valuable."

"Your reputation."

"He would have sent her to jail, ruined her life."

"So you ruined his."

She peered at me under thick lids. "Do you have children?"

I thought of my brother Colton, who would have turned thirty-four this year if my father hadn't murdered him and my mother. "You know I don't."

"Gary Hudson forgot the first rule about families."

"What's that?"

"Never come between a mother and her child."

I closed my eyes and watched the red lights of the emergency vehicles strobe across my lids. "I saw you after Susan Thompson was killed. You don't murder people, no matter who they hurt."

She drew a deep breath into that birdlike breast of hers. "I have Stage IV ovarian cancer. It has metastasized to other organs. It is far too advanced for surgery. I refuse to go through any more of those debilitating chemo and radiation treatments. I want to spend my remaining days at home, not hooked to some machine."

I groped for a way to respond. "How long do you have?"

"A few months, at best."

"And the agency?"

"Melissa will take over."

I looked at the huddled figure. She seemed to absorb the darkness around her. "Do you think she's ready?"

"She'll have to be."

I nodded. "Why tell me?"

"You won't rest until you've gotten to the bottom of this. You always put your grandfather first. I would expect you of all people to understand."

"What's to keep me from going to the police?"

"At this point, it's my word against yours and, in this town, mine counts. I said your obsession with Phil would come back to haunt you. You are the little girl who cried wolf one too many times."

"That's not going to help Melissa."

"All you have tried to do since you moved here is destroy my family, first my husband and now my daughter. You've finally succeeded. I hope you're happy."

"Far from it," I said.

She left to argue with Trooper Robinson about her car. She told him her daughter was in shock, she needed to go to the hospital. No, she said, they didn't want to ride in the ambulance. She wanted to take her daughter in her own car. Robinson said it had to stay where it was, until the accident reconstruction team arrived. He said he'd call a tow truck when they'd finished.

"Don't be ridiculous," Casey barked. "The tire's barely off the road."

Before either of us could react, Casey marched to the SUV, clicked the remote starter and slid inside.

Convinced she was going to flee, I stepped in front of the car. Casey hit the gas, the big grill of the SUV leaping forward as she tried to crush me between her bumper and the back of the Prius. I dove for the ditch and rolled as bumpers splintered and showered me with debris.

Casey flung the car in reverse. The troopers trained their weapons on her windshield and yelled, "Out of the car! Now!"

32.

"SHE DIDN'T THINK I'd live to tell," I said as we sat on the dock of the Spanish Point marina, the three of us—Rae, Sugar Bear and I—waiting for Walter's sailboat to return.

"You have to testify?" Rae asked.

"I doubt it. Both of them seem in a race to confess."

Almost mid-October and less than three weeks from the official start of the season and it still felt like summer. The sun shone and a westerly breeze ruffled the leaves. The first wave of tourists had arrived. They crowded the restaurants and combed the marina and haunted its statues in search of the perfect selfie. No one bothered the basin where Tamika had drowned. There was no statue, no marker. Everything looked normal. Just another day in paradise.

As if she were thinking along the same line, Rae gave us a snippet of an Otis Redding song, "Dock of the Bay." She skipped most of verse but punched out the line about nothing coming her way.

I'd brought a backpack and, leaning against it, placed a hand on Sugar Bear's head. It felt soft and warm. "Don't listen to the mad woman." I'd brought the dog to greet Walter's Louie. Or maybe because I felt afraid to sit here, even with a friend, not knowing how Walter would react.

Rae had tagged along for moral support. She'd actually run a brush through her hair and looked presentable. We both did, the scrapes on my face, arm and leg healing smartly.

She broke the silence. "So what's story, or do I have to wait for the movie?"

I hesitated.

"I know, you can't talk. You're sworn to secrecy. You've taken a sacred blood oath."

"Cheryl told me in confidence."

"Cheryl the cop."

"My neighbor."

"You've got friends in low places."

It was the first time I'd heard her joke in a while and it sounded good.

"You want the truth?"

"No," she said. "I want the politicians' buffet of all the lies I can eat."

"All right. There's some guesswork but this is what the police think happened. Melissa invited Tamika to dinner at the house she shares with her mother on Spanish Key. They were supposed to discuss the news reports about the two projects. Tamika supposedly said she was too busy for dinner but could meet them after. She knew they lived on the Gulf and mentioned that she'd lived here for two years and hadn't gone out on the water. Melissa said she had access to a boat and they could watch the sunset from the pass between the barrier islands."

Rae interrupted. "That's not what you said earlier, about what Laine said about the boat."

"Casey told me she invited Tamika to tour the projects from the water, but I'd put money on Melissa's version."

"I wouldn't trust either of them to give me the time of day."

I bit my lip. She waved me on.

"So they agreed to meet at the marina and parked in the lot." I hooked a thumb over my shoulder. "The boat is Phil's old runabout. He sold it to Stefan the harbormaster, who maintained the craft and took the mayor's donors on fishing trips. Melissa and Tamika motored out of the harbor and into the pass, where they tried to round the key. But Melissa doesn't know a yardarm from a yardstick."

"Yardarms are on square-riggers. I thought this was a motorboat."

"Who's telling this story?"

"Carry on."

Sugar Bear licked my hand.

"Thank you," I said. "What I meant to say, for the more literal-minded among us, was that Melissa was an inexperienced pilot. Because a storm had just passed, the water was rougher than she expected. The wind was blowing from the west, seas at three to four feet, and the boat struggled against the chop. Tamika supposedly confessed that she'd never learned to swim and insisted they turn back. Melissa promised that, once they got to the bay, things would calm down."

Sugar Bear turned three times and lay on the grass, her head in my lap. I scratched her neck and resumed the epic tale.

"They got to the mouth of the harbor and started arguing about whether Tamika was going to call for an investigation into the report on Vertex. Melissa hadn't weighed anchor, so the boat was rocking. She said that Tamika stumbled and started to fall overboard. Melissa grabbed the first thing she could reach, the necklace. Tamika went under and disappeared. Melissa panicked. She managed to get the boat to the dock but, because she didn't tie it down, it drifted."

Rae said, "She panicked."

I nodded. "Once she got ashore, Melissa called her mom, who told her to come home. Casey then drove to the marina with the idea of wiping down the boat, but there was too much activity. No need to sanitize Tamika's car because Melissa was never in it, so Casey left. Meanwhile, another owner, afraid the boat would scrape his craft, called the harbormaster."

"Who broke out the Mr. Clean?"

"Stefan—he's the harbormaster—secures the boat. A little later, the body appears and a yacht owner calls police. That's when we arrived."

"The body washed in pretty quick," Rae said.

"There was a strong tide, and every boat that passed created a wake."

"And nobody spotted a hysterical woman running from the boat."

"There are no cameras at the marina except near the restaurant. The police had to do a door-to-door search. They found a witness who said he saw a man in a baseball cap who struggled with the boat before leaving it to drift. He said it was dark and he was too far away to see the face."

Rae asked what Melissa was wearing.

"She wore long pants and a man's shirt and tucked her hair under a baseball cap."

"That's where you got the idea the mayor was involved."

"Same height and build. Because of the cap, the witness couldn't see the hair."

"So they did take you seriously," Rae said.

"Eventually," I said. "I think Tony pushed it."

"You believe that story?" Rae asked. "That the two of them just wanted to put the fear of God in her?"

"I don't think they intended to hurt her."

"I've got no sympathy," Rae said. "They let her drown."

"They did."

"So there's no way to tie the mayor into all this."

"He was at a fundraiser. A hundred people can give him an alibi."

Rae wanted to know how Hud got involved.

"Mother and daughter live in a gated community that requires barcode stickers on the residents' cars. The gatehouse logged Melissa and Casey coming and going the night Tamika drowned. Hud is friends with one of the guards. From the logs he inferred that either of the women could have been on the water at the time of Tamika's death."

"And Casey, who's generous with the bonuses at Christmas, finds out this guy's been minding her business."

"The guards told her someone had been asking questions. They provided a name, contact information and a description. When

Hud called for a meeting to discuss something for their mutual benefit, Casey had a plan."

"Who hit the guy?"

"Melissa," I said. "Casey wanted to take the rap but it may not fly. FHP is in charge of motor vehicle deaths. Their reconstruction team is pretty thorough."

"So where are they now?"

"Where you'd expect two rich women to be," I said. "Out on bail."

"What's the charge?"

"Involuntary manslaughter and criminal attempt for Tamika. Cheryl said Melissa could get the full ride for Hud."

"Good," Rae said. "I hope they both hang. What about the mayor? They nail him for anything?"

"No. The fact that he used to own the boat could cost him a couple of votes but he's outspending his opponent ten to one. He might be tarnished but he'll survive."

"To quote that great philosopher Meatloaf, two out of three ain't bad. I can tell by that look you don't think so."

"If I'd gone there a little earlier, before Casey and Melissa got to him."

"It's like with Ryan—would'a, could'a, should'a. It'll drive you nuts. Pretty soon, you're taking on the sins of the world."

As the boats drifted in and out of harbor, I let that bit of wisdom rattle through my mind.

Rae interrupted the thought. "What happens with the agency?"

"Laine & Company? Who knows?"

"You could run it."

I laughed. "Run me out of town, is more like it."

"Those towers. They're still going up, right?"

"Code enforcement crawled all over the buildings and hasn't found a single crack, which is good news for the people living there."

Rae wanted to know about Vertex.

"My guess is the city will order new soundings to cover its ass."

"But I'm gonna lose another bar."

I reached to touch her arm and knuckled her cast instead. "It looks that way."

She stared through the forest of masts into the gleaming bay. "That's a lot of loose ends, kiddo."

Walter's favorite expression popped into my head and I gave it voice. "It is what it is."

"When's the boat supposed to get here?"

"Sometime this afternoon."

"And you're going to sit on your keester until it does?"

I petted Sugar Bear. "What else can I do?"

She pointed to my hair. "I'd start by ditching the highlights."

"Too SoCal?"

"Life's hard enough," she said. "You don't wanna work at being somebody else."

"You're just full of advice, aren't you?"

"Any who." Grunting, Rae used the cast to lever her body from the dock. "I gotta get to work, if the place still exists." She must have read something in my face because she paused. "I know three's a crowd, but I can stay if you want."

"Thanks, but you've seen enough raw emotion for a lifetime."

With a salute, Rae walked to the parking lot and ignited her bike. I dug a bowl and bottle of water from the backpack and gave Sugar Bear a drink. As she lapped, I thought about fresh starts, and what I'd change this time around. Deciding whether to stay at Laine & Company topped the list. Whether Phil Cunningham or a new owner ran the place, I was done. I might even consider another career. But the money was good, and even a decade after the Great Recession, Spanish Point continued to boom. There seemed no end to the demand for sun and surf, and the property that made those dreams real.

If my professional life was uncertain, my personal life felt even less so. I could apologize to Mitch and Tony for incessantly berating them. I could even take a sabbatical from men—for their own protection. Both ideas seemed like New Year's resolutions, easy to make, impossible to keep.

A two-masted rig caught my eye. Sails down, powered by a small outboard, the *Mary Beth* chugged toward the dock. I rested a hand on Sugar Bear's head. Walter must have stopped on the way to collect his Labrador because Louie surged to the bow and barked out a greeting. Then Walter appeared, tall and rugged in his rusty T-shirt and baseball cap. And I knew, at least for the moment, that everything would be all right.

Acknowledgements

Thank you to the members of the Bradenton Writers Group—Jean Muccini, Lynn Purple, George Thomas and Eric Sheridan Wyatt. Throughout the series, your generosity and insight have helped to bring the character of CW McCoy to life.

Books by Jeff Widmer

Fiction
The CW McCoy Series
Peak Season
Tourist in Paradise
Curb Appeal
Permanent Vacation

The Brinker Series
Mr. Mayhem
Mr. Magic

Standalone novels
Born Under a Bad Sign (Spring 2019)

Nonfiction
The Spirit of Swiftwater
Riding with the Blues

About the Author

Jeff Widmer has worked as a dishwasher, surveyor, guitarist, journalist, and marketing professional. He is the author of the CW McCoy and the Brinker series of crime novels as well as numerous works of nonfiction. A native of Northeast Pennsylvania, he lives in Sarasota, Florida.

Connect

If you enjoyed this book, please share a review on your favorite merchant or social-media site. And join me online at:

Website
http://www.jeffwidmer.com/

Author page
https://www.amazon.com/author/jeffwidmer

Facebook
https://www.facebook.com/jeff.widmer

Flickr
http://www.flickr.com/photos/jrwidmer/

Goodreads
https://www.goodreads.com/jeffwidmer

Instagram
http://instagram.com/jrwidmer/

LinkedIn
http://www.linkedin.com/in/jeffwidmer

Pinterest
http://pinterest.com/jrwidmer/

Twitter
@jrwidmer

YouTube
https://www.youtube.com/user/widworks

Born Under a Bad Sign

Read the exciting first chapter of Jeff Widmer's new standalone novel, *Born Under a Bad Sign*, available in the spring of 2019. Set in the turbulent Sixties just weeks before the Woodstock Music & Art Fair, the book tells the story of two lovers fighting for their dreams, and their lives.

1.

FROM BEYOND THE hills came a jagged flash of light. Elizabeth Reed counted five seconds before the sound rumbled across the infield of the raceway, this makeshift venue for the largest outdoor rock concert on the East Coast. Another flash, and another ripple of thunder. In an improvised call and response, the crowd echoed its approval. The tower that held the lights and PA system trembled. So did Elizabeth's arms and legs. She let the dizziness pass and, willing her stomach to settle, tucked both cameras under her arms and climbed to the sky.

The warm-up band had just finished, the announcer promising that Orwell, fresh off its national tour, would soon take the stage. A wall of people surged forward. Despite the scalding July heat, this was the group's homecoming and the locals had turned out in force, thousands of ragged kids with beards and muumuus, jostling each other in a fog of beer and smoke. Two years after Monterey Pop and the festival had come of age. So had the band.

The tower swayed enough to cause Elizabeth to question her bravado. Despite the knot in her stomach, she climbed past speakers and spotlights for a better view of the makeshift stage, a plywood floor laid across a half-dozen flatbed trailers. The platform had been hastily constructed for the festival, the biggest in Pennsylvania's Minisink Valley and a warm-up for one she'd heard could be even bigger, next month's Woodstock Music & Art Fair in nearby New York.

That was the real object of the evening's performance, a final rehearsal for Orwell and its leader, Hayden Quinn, the guitarist *Rolling Stone* had called the next Jimi Hendrix, the man that Elizabeth, fresh out of high school, had followed halfway across the country as the band's unofficial photographer. It was make or break time for the group. The band's manager, Elizabeth's Uncle Morey, had invited the man organizing Woodstock, Michael Lang, to attend the concert. So far, she hadn't seen anyone fitting Lang's description.

As the wind rose to meet the night, Elizabeth realized that, if the crowd pressed closer, the tower could tip. Since her dizziness disappeared if she didn't look down, she focused on the distance, tracking the Delaware as it wandered between Pennsylvania and New Jersey like a nomad, flowing freely despite the government's effort to dam the river and drown her family's farm. With the telephoto lens, she could isolate her property, snug in the rich bottomland of the valley. Camera in hand, river and fields spread below, she felt exhausted, scared, and ridiculously happy.

Voices below startled her. Dressed in black, two members of the security crew waved her from the tower. The yelling morphed into the sound of hammering. Against the raw wood of the stage, Tommy Reed nailed cardboard cylinders to rows of two-by-tens, preparing the fireworks for the evening's finale. He seemed dwarfed by the munitions.

When the sound system kicked in with a recording of "Crossroads," Elizabeth gripped the metal pipes to maintain her balance. Despite the rush of adrenaline, her arms ached from lugging the heavy Nikons all day. With a normal lens, the weight seemed bearable. But when loaded with a zoom and a motor drive, the outfit felt as if it weighed as much as a bale of hay. Before she descended, she snapped a picture of Tommy as he wired his makeshift rig, the camera hot and slippery in her hands. Heaven help them if she dropped it on his head.

As soon as she landed, the security officers assumed their positions in front of the stage while the roadies assembled the last of the equipment. Her older brother Robbie frowned as he arranged cymbals and tightened the drumheads, his rusty hair in a deliberately unhip buzzcut. Reaching above his head, Cordell White plugged his bass into a stack of amplifiers and plucked a few notes. Unlike Robbie, who wore his usual white T-shirt and shorts, Del had dressed for show in leather pants, a jacket of purple satin, and a high-crowned Navajo hat with a yellow plume. Both of them looked frustrated, or mad.

Tommy caught her eye and jerked his head toward the edge of the stage. He, too, appeared angry, a look that was highlighted by chapped lips, hair the color of licorice, and a nose as sharp as a chisel. The only festive thing about him was the tie-dyed headband.

"Hey, Cuz," she said, drawing a face that signaled either irritation or fatigue.

He smelled of oil and mint. As usual, he wore sunglasses so dark that she wondered how he could see to connect the fireworks. Pecking him on the cheek, she took in the rows of rockets, mortars, and Roman candles that crowded both sides of the stage and felt a twinge of concern. "Aren't they a little close?"

Tommy scratched his back with a screwdriver. "Close?"

"To the band."

Another crack of thunder and Tommy dragged a tarp over the pods. "Wait and see."

As security stopped a ginger-haired man flashing press credentials, Elizabeth regained the tower. One by one, the members of Orwell wandered onto the stage to a cascade of applause. Robbie positioned his cymbals, Del and Quinn hunched over tuning pegs, and Mattie, jiggling her ample ass, asked the crowd how they were doing. As the band struck its first tectonic chord, the audience thundered their approval.

Mattie belted out the first number with a ferocity that shook the towers, all trace of her Southern accent lost in the ricochet of sound. Robbie thrashed as if he were drowning in one of the cow ponds on the family farm. Even Del, who usually bobbed in place, stalked the boards, his face a darkening cloud.

Quinn followed with a scorching lead that featured a collision of Bach, Thelonious Monk, and Hendrix. Shirtless now and barefoot, he played with a single-mindedness akin to religious devotion, prowling the stage, slashing his guitar, bending strings until they threatened to snap. He hammered the neck with both hands as if playing a piano, the sound a frenetic cross between Paganini and Robert Johnson, the shaman who'd sold his soul to the devil for his talent.

From her perch, she tracked the band, feeling more than hearing the smack of the mirror as it lifted to admit the light, the whir of the motor drive as it advanced the frames. *Pace yourself*, she thought, *or you'll run out of film.*

Like a tsunami, the intensity of the music grew, Quinn hurtling his body into the wave of sound, his head bowed, shoulders hunched, fingers on fire. Dreadlocks flew as he reared, face twisted in ecstasy, the notes tracking across his lips. No matter how many times she'd seen the show, Elizabeth felt stunned, and not just by the acoustical acrobatics. With the flick of his fingers, Quinn guided the music from brave to anxious to calm. Elizabeth felt warmth and humor, sadness and pity, and so much in between. It astonished her that anyone could convey such emotion without the use of a single word.

The band continued the pace, blazing through songs as if racing to an uncertain end. By the close of the set, their faces shone with euphoria and sweat. Robbie raised his sticks, caught the eye of Quinn and Del, and they miraculously finished on the same beat, even as Tommy launched the first volley of fireworks, burning the night in a shower of red and gold.

The musicians filtered off stage, waited a beat, and returned to a swelling ovation. With a deep bow, and a nod from Mattie, they launched into one of the medleys Quinn had arranged as an encore. Even before Elizabeth traced their faces through the telephoto, she could tell that, as the music grew more frantic, they struggled to hear. Hitting the final chorus, Mattie looked over her shoulder as if she were lost in the woods. Robbie buried his head in his drum kit. Del and Quinn traded places, Del moving to the monitors along the wing while Quinn arched over the stage to listen to the PA speakers.

The music had grown so loud that Elizabeth could barely feel the vibration through the camera body as the motor drive cranked through another roll of film, thirty-six exposures in a matter of seconds before she hunched to reload.

This time, the band didn't leave the stage. They bowed slightly, as if they'd expended so much energy they had little left for movement, before launching into the second encore, a reprise of their single, "Bomb Babies," that ended in a cataclysmic version of Tchaikovsky's *1812 Overture*. Quinn had shortened the piece for maximum impact and, when he nodded, Tommy let loose with his final volley.

From the corner of the viewfinder, Elizabeth watched the skyrockets arc into the night and explode in phosphorescent swirls. She grabbed a shot of Tommy, who timed the bursts to coincide with the downbeat. As the encore hit its crescendo, he quickened the pace, unleashing a white-hot assault that mimicked the original cannon fire. The band fed off the energy, Quinn and Robbie flailing, Del leaning dangerously close to the fireworks while Mattie spread her arms to embrace the crowd.

Then, as Elizabeth lifted the camera to her face, the stage flashed with a blinding light and the world exploded.

Made in the USA
Columbia, SC
16 December 2018